House of Lies and Sorrow

FAE OF REWYTH BOOK 1

EMILY BLACKWOOD

Cover Design by Moonpress www.moonpress.co

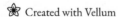 Created with Vellum

For the readers who get bored with normal.

CHAPTER 1
Jade

"How do you think he'll kill you?" Tessa asked me.

I continued focusing on the knot that I was tying, even though I was certain the blood had rushed from my face. "I'm not really sure. I haven't thought about it," I lied.

Of course I had thought about how I was going to die.

I had pictured all the ways he could end my meaningless life.

Would it be as simple as a dagger to the chest?

Or something less merciful?

But my sister never saw me as weak. She wasn't about to start now. I put a joking smile on my face before I added, "I wonder if he'll do it himself, or if he'll send someone else to finish his dirty work."

Tessa leaned in with the same smile she always wore while gossiping. At least my upcoming death was important news to her. "Hopefully he does it himself. I heard he's handsome as sin."

I shoved her away playfully, not daring to drop the smile that I forced onto my face. "You've been listening to too many rumors, little sister. Those big ears of yours will get you into trouble. We both know nobody knows anything about the Prince of Shadows."

Tessa didn't respond. She looked down at her own knot she was tying, studying it closely. Except she wasn't still tying it, either. She had dropped the rope into her lap and had begun picking at her fingernails. The silence grew heavier with every second.

"You never know, Jade. Maybe he'll end up really liking you. Maybe he'll fall madly in love and he'll protect you with his life." Her voice took a turn from light and playful to serious and emotional. "You have to try. You have to *try* to survive. Promise me you'll try to make him like you? That you'll fight?"

Her large, deep eyes were searching my face for an answer. They were searching for any slither of hope that I wasn't being sent to my imminent death.

But I knew the truth. I was being sent into the fae lands to marry one of the fae princes.

And if that wasn't bad enough, I was going to marry the Prince of Shadows. The merciless, deadly prince that waltzed through this world with no consequences.

And like every human wife he had before me, I was going to be killed.

Any other scenario would be a useless attempt at having hope.

There was no way around it. I was going to die.

But I smiled at my sister anyway. "Of course, I'll try, Tessa. I'll do everything I can. You know I'm not one to give up easily."

She seemed pleased with my words, and she quickly resumed tending to her own knot.

Tessa was a worrier. I knew that's why my father had chosen me, along with many other things.

She was softer. She was likable. She didn't have sharp edges and scars. She didn't come with damage. She was *perfect*.

I, on the other hand, was not even close to perfect. I was damaged.

I was easily expendable. Which was why I was being sent to my death.

Okay, I was being sent to my marriage. But what was the difference?

"Give me that," I demanded after watching her fumble with the rope a few times. She gave it to me without hesitating and watched in awe as I tied the perfect knot in a matter of seconds. "Here," I said, handing it back to her. "You're going to have to learn this type of thing when I'm gone. We all know father isn't any help."

She giggled again, but it didn't quite reach her eyes. "I know, I know. I wish you could stay a little longer to help me."

"I wish I could stay longer, too. Unfortunately for

us, time is not our friend. We've put this off for long enough."

"I still don't understand why it has to be you!" Tessa said, her emotions seeping into every word. Thick tears began welling in her eyes. "Why can't someone else marry the fae prince! Why does it have to be you?"

I dropped the knot and pulled her into my arms. She didn't know the details about the deal my father had made with the fae king. His life for mine. I took a deep breath and told myself to calm down. Just thinking about it made my blood boil. How could he be so reckless? Of course, he had gotten caught. And when the king learned that he had two daughters, they made a deal.

My life for his.

Of course, it wasn't me that they wanted. I was just the one father picked. To nobody's surprise, either.

But Tessa didn't know that part, and I certainly was not about to tell her. It's not like she would jump up to take my place or anything, but she would at least feel guilty.

At least I hoped she would.

But even if Tessa was ignorant, useless, skinny, and slightly selfish, I was determined to keep her safe. She had experienced enough hardships in this life, even though I had done everything in my power to protect her.

And if this was going to help protect her, I would do it with a smile on my face. A fake smile, at least.

"It's getting dark," I said after a few minutes. "I'm

going for one more hunt before tomorrow. I won't be long. Go inside and make sure father is asleep by the time I get back."

"Okay," she agreed, rolling her eyes. "Be careful out there!"

"I always am," I said before grabbing the rest of our rope and throwing it over my shoulder, bending down to kiss her cheek before turning my back on our cottage and heading toward the tree line.

My mind was racing. From the day I learned of the deal my father had made with the fae king, I knew I would die for his mistakes. I just always thought I would have more time.

Now, I had only a handful of hours left in my life.

But there wasn't time to panic. Tessa needed food. My biggest fear wasn't dying. It wasn't marrying one of the most evil creatures on the planet, and it wasn't traveling to the fae lands.

My biggest fear was Tessa dying because of me.

If I died–when I died, Tessa would have nothing. I had tried to prepare her for this, but there was only so much I could do. My father was nothing but a drunken burden. He was no provider. He was no father. Ever since I could carry a knife, I would wander into the forest and gather food for Tessa and me. Without it, we certainly would have starved to death. Not like that was rare in the human lands, but still.

I was all Tessa had. I wasn't going to let her die, too.

I buried my emotions and focused on the land around me. We were lucky to live close enough to so much empty land, making it easier to hunt for food instead of paying for meat at the markets.

Saints, everyone knew we didn't have the money for that.

I never caught anything too big. Mostly rabbits with snares that Tessa and I would make. But it kept us alive. It kept us fed, which was better than most people who lived in these lands. It wasn't rare to see children so skinny that you could count every bone. It also wasn't rare to be killed over a loaf of bread if a family was desperate enough.

Tessa would need as much as possible after I left if she was going to make it.

The ground turned from the plowed dirt path to the full, leafy jungle that surrounded our land. Walking my familiar path deep into the forest, I approached the snares I had set up yesterday.

Please have something, I silently pleaded. *Anything*.

My old, worn boots crunched on every dead leaf and broken branch beneath me. Those were the sounds that had grown to comfort me all these years later. This was the place I learned to find my peace.

Relief flooded my body once I saw the dead rabbit I had caught.

I wasn't leaving empty handed. That was something.

There were many nights when I hadn't been so lucky. I pushed away the memories of Tessa crying from hunger, my father screaming that I was no good to the family.

I began releasing the prey from the trap, pushing away any emotions that came with it.

I was nine when I killed my first. My father had forced me with him on one of his hunts. He used to love hunting. That was before my mother died, of course.

The only thing he loved now was drinking.

They don't deserve to live more than you do, he said. *They die or your sister will starve to death. Pick one.*

I shot an arrow through its tiny body and cried for the rest of the day. How cruel life was, to create something so fragile and give it no chance at surviving.

A deep growl rumbled the air around me, piercing through the silence. The hair on the back of my neck stuck up. A few feet away stood the largest wolf I had ever seen, eyeing the rabbit that he had thought was his.

He was going to attack me.

Perhaps this was how I was going to die. I had to admit, it sounded better than marriage.

"Easy there," I whispered under my breath. "Is this what you want?" I held the rabbit out between us, trying to draw the wolf's attention from me to the meat.

The wolf bared his teeth and growled again.

I guess he was really pissed.

"Take it and go," I whispered again, as if he could understand what I was saying anyway. Every inch of my body was telling me to run. But I was no fool.

And I knew that wolves never traveled alone.

Human footsteps on the forest floor approached

behind me, but I didn't dare take my eyes off the creature. It wasn't all that rare for other hunters to run into me out here. If I was lucky, whoever it was would scare the wolf away.

"What in the Saints are you doing?" a deep male voice behind me made me jump.

"Stop! Don't move!" I hissed, whipping my gaze between the towering wolf and the strange, hooded man behind me. He stood with his hands in his pockets, clearly not a threat.

"Whatever you say," he said in a casual tone that made me even angrier than I already was.

I focused back on the wolf. If I could get his attention onto the rabbit, I could throw it into the trees and get out of here.

But then I would be empty handed. Tessa would be hungry. All of this would be for nothing.

"It's you or me," I said to the hungry beast, "and I'm afraid I have a family to feed." I tucked the rabbit into my satchel and backed away slowly.

Which only made the wolf let out a deep, blood-curdling howl toward the sky.

A low laughter filled the air behind me. "I think you've angered him," the man said. I kept stepping backward away from the wolf and in the direction of the man.

I didn't care. I had dealt with many men in my life. Men were nothing compared to a hungry pack of wolves.

Although they often liked to think otherwise.

"Shut up," I mumbled in his direction. The wolf stepped forward, following my every move.

And then another wolf followed behind it.

Shit.

There had to be more hiding in the bushes, and they were no longer interested in the rabbit.

They were interested in me.

The man behind me knew it too. He gave a quiet noise of satisfaction.

I unsheathed the knife, holding it out in front of me.

"Come on then," I said to the wolf, loud enough for my audience to hear. "If you're going to kill me, do it already!"

I didn't care that I sounded crazy. This was my last night alive, anyway. If the wolf decided to attack, I at least had a chance at killing one of them before they killed me.

At least my death wouldn't be for nothing.

"You should probably get behind me," the man said. "Unless you want to be dinner for about five wolves."

"Get away from me," I said, continuing to step backward. I knew I was just a few feet from him. The wolves were pushing me closer and closer.

I took another step backward. Then another.

When I took one more step, I found myself pressed against the man's chest.

He didn't touch me, though. Just laughed silently. I could tell by the way his body shook against my back.

The wolves didn't seem to pay him any attention. He wasn't the one that had stolen their dinner.

A third wolf came into view, snapping its jaw just inches from my legs. I jumped back on instinct, further into the stranger's body.

Coward, I thought to myself. I twisted the knife in my hand, gripping tightly. Would it be enough? If these wolves lunged, would my knife protect me? By the looks of it, it would take much more than a knife to take one of them down.

Seconds later, I had no choice.

The wolf in front of me lunged, and my body reacted without my permission. I didn't cower this time. I lunged myself forward, knife out, aiming for the wolf's throat.

A mixture of limbs, fur, and claws hit the forest floor. I was waiting for the piercing pain of teeth to impale me, but it never came.

And my knife never made contact, either.

An aggressive, alpha growl rumbled through the still air right before strong hands pulled me from the floor, dragging me backward. My knife slipped from my grip, but the hands kept dragging me away.

And the wolves didn't follow.

"Are you out of your damn mind?" The stranger hissed into my ear, dropping me to the floor. "You're going to get yourself killed!"

I scrambled to my feet, ready to fight with my bare hands if I needed to. That knife wouldn't have helped much, anyway.

"They're going to–" I started, but froze.

The wolves, who were just seconds away from ripping me apart, were now backing away. Each of their heads bowed and their tails were now tucked between their legs.

Not because of me, though. No– they were all focused on the man to my left.

I had never seen anything like it.

As soon as the animals turned their attention onto him, the energy in the forest changed.

What was he doing?

He stepped forward once, and the wolves scattered completely. He must have known some secret to deter the wolves that I didn't know. That was the only explanation.

That, or the fact that the man was an absolute giant.

I was of average height, but this man towered over me. And his wide shoulders told me that he was certainly strong enough to fight one of the beasts if given the opportunity.

"What was that?" I asked. I hated the way my heart was pounding in my chest. I was too close to death to be afraid of it. "What did you do?"

The man turned to me, and I saw his face for the first time. He didn't look much older than I, but he had sharp, mature features that matched the clear leanness of his body. His dark hair stuck out under his hood, even blacker than my own.

I was certain I had never seen him before. I would have remembered.

"What makes you think you can take on a pack of wolves with your bare hands?" he asked. His voice was dripping with anger.

"That's none of your business. And it wasn't with my bare hands. I was armed," I said, crossing my arms.

The man laughed. "Right. You're lucky I was here, or you would have been slaughtered."

"Excuse me?"

"What? You think that sad excuse for a dagger was going to save you? I've seen a pack of wolves much smaller than that take down an entire lioness, sweetheart. Don't bite off more than you can chew next time."

I was actually speechless. Who the Saints did this guy think he was? He knew nothing about me or my experience with hunting.

He continued anyway. "A lady should not be wandering the forest alone after the sun goes down," he said. "It's dangerous, as I'm sure you know by now."

He was still standing way too close to me, but I didn't back away. He was trying to intimidate me, and by the smirk he wore on his face, he knew it.

"Do not speak down to me," I said, rolling my shoulders backward. "I am not a child. My family needs food, and I am providing it. You can mind your own business next time."

He laughed and shook his head. "That's a lot of

confidence coming from someone who nearly just died. You're welcome, by the way."

"I don't need your help," I spat. The darkness hid the embarrassment rising to my face. I hoped so, at least.

I turned away from the stranger and began walking toward the edge of the forest. Going back for my knife would have been no use. I wouldn't need it anymore, anyway. Not after tomorrow.

"You provide food for your entire family?" he asked, catching up beside me.

I don't know why I felt the need to answer him, but I did anyway. "My sister, Tessa. My dad's a useless drunk. Someone has to put food on the table."

A flash of something crossed his dark features, but it passed before I could identify it.

"Did you make that rabbit trap yourself?" he asked, continuing the interrogation. How long had he been watching me? Annoyance crept into my body. Was he serious? Following me into the forest to embarrass me, taunt me, and start casual conversation as if we were friends?

"Look," I said, stopping and turning to face him. "I don't know who you are or what you're doing out here, but it's probably best for both of us if you go home and leave me alone. And if you're a creep who thinks he can take advantage of a young woman, just know that that knife isn't just for rabbits. And it wouldn't be the first time I've used it on a man."

I was angry. My heart was beating into my ears.

But the man just smiled in amusement, crossing his hands over his chest and leaning on the nearby tree.

"Okay, Jade," he said. "I'll leave you be, then. My apologies for interrupting your clearly under-control hunting trip."

"How do you know my name?" I asked, stepping forward. "Who are you?"

He paused in thought, as if he were debating on whether or not to answer me.

"I know your name because you are marrying the Prince of Shadows tomorrow. Everyone knows your name, Jade Farrow."

"That's not true," I said. My heart sank to my stomach, dread creeping into my senses. "Nobody knows about that."

"You're very wrong," he said. "It's all anyone's been speaking about for weeks."

"You're not from around here," I said. "I've never seen you before. How did you find out about my marriage?"

He smiled in amusement again.

He was taller than any man in my village, stronger than any of them, and a complete stranger.

A chill ran through me. Could he be a fae? In the human lands?

I shook my head. No. It was impossible. He didn't even have wings. The darkness hid most of his features, but I didn't see pointed ears, either. They looked normal, with a small silver piercing on his left ear.

"Nervous about something?" he asked. His calmness and cockiness were doing nothing to help my growing agitation.

"Yes," I answered. "I'm nervous about how damn creepy you're being. If you won't answer my questions, then I suppose I'll be on my way. It was *not* nice to meet you, stranger."

I turned to continue walking, but he pushed himself off the tree and blocked my path.

"You're being sent to marry a fae prince," he repeated. *It wasn't a question.*

I lifted my chin. My mind swarmed with the possibilities of what he could possibly want from me. Did he need me for leverage? Or did he hate the fae so much he wanted to kill anyone associated? This man might have been a stranger, but I was not going to show him fear. Not on my last day alive.

"No," I said with all the confidence and power I could muster. "I'm being sent to be *killed* by a fae prince. Not much of a difference, though."

For the first time during this entire interaction, the man looked shocked.

"What, you're surprised?" I asked. "If you know enough to know that I am being married off, then you should know that every human who marries the mysterious Prince of Shadows ends up dead."

"Those are rumors," he said, suddenly defensive.

"Maybe," I replied. "But rumors start from somewhere."

"I have a good feeling about this. You will not die

tomorrow, Jade Farrow. I wish you a long and happy marriage to your mysterious Prince of Shadows."

His words were respectful and cordial, but I nearly laughed in his face. A marriage to the Prince of Shadows had no hope of being happy. *I* had no hope.

Death would be easier.

"Sure," I said after a few seconds. "Whatever you say…"

"Mal. My name's Mal."

"Well, *Mal,* I should get going. Big day tomorrow and all."

I'm not sure why I was expecting him to protest, but the tiniest amount of disappointment crept into my chest when he nodded his head and moved away so I could pass.

"I'm sure I will see you again soon, Jade," he said as I walked away. I ignored the butterflies that ignited in my stomach, likely from the sudden nerves about the realization of what would happen tomorrow.

Mal was never going to see me again. Tonight was my last night alive.

CHAPTER 2
Jade

My father was awake when I made it back to the house.

Not good.

His slurred, temperamental voice carried into the street, followed by Tessa's crying. I changed pace into a run.

"What's going on?" I said, storming through the front door. My father, clearly drunk, was pacing in the kitchen. Tessa had cowered herself into a corner, arms across her body and tears streaming down her face.

If he laid a hand on her, even a finger, I was going to kill him.

"Are you okay?" I asked Tessa, running to her and blocking her line of sight with my body. "Did he hit you?"

She shook her head. "Then what's going on?"

She opened her mouth to speak but the only thing that came out was a stifled sob.

My father shattered something behind me, mumbling something that I couldn't understand.

I turned my back to Tessa but made sure to keep her protected.

"You should be asleep," I yelled to him. He staggered forward, shirtless, and nearly tripped over nothing.

"Don't tell me what to do, girl," he slurred as he caught himself on the kitchen table. "I'm your father. I'll go to bed when I please."

My body stiffened. "You're drunk. It's late."

"I know how late it is. I am not an idiot, despite what you believe. You look down on me, you treat me like garbage. But I am the leader of this household. Show some respect, both of you!"

Tessa was still crying behind me. "Go to your room," I whispered to her, making sure my father wasn't paying attention as she slipped by in a hurry.

I hated that she saw him this way. I hated that she had to endure his behavior, and I hated that after tomorrow I wouldn't be here to help her.

My father reached for a mug of ale that likely came home with him from whatever tavern he had wasted away inside of all day. I grabbed the mug of ale from his hand and slammed it back onto the kitchen table, causing liquid to splash over the both of us.

"That's enough," I demanded.

"It's enough when I say it's enough," he responded, but his words strung together.

"Just go to sleep!" I said, feeling my temper unraveling. "Isn't it bad enough that you scared Tessa? Can you just for once be a good father and not ruin everything?"

He considered me for a moment, then clenched his jaw. "You disrespectful brat. After everything I've done for you, too."

"Everything you've *done* for me?" I asked. "Please enlighten me on all of the great things you've done for me. I'm dying to know. Especially after I've kept this family alive all these years."

"*You've* kept us alive?" he spat. "You would be nothing without me. Nothing! I taught you everything you know, child!"

"You taught me what a deadbeat father looks like. You taught me that I have nobody in this life to count on but myself. And when I die tomorrow, which I will, it will be *your* fault. So thank you, father, for everything you've done. I apologize that I have not been more grateful." I spun on my heel and turned toward my bedroom.

"You are marrying a prince, Jade. A prince! You *should* be thanking me!"

"Thanking you? You want me to thank you for ruining my life?"

Before I could back away, my father slapped me hard across my face.

It wasn't the first time he had hit me. But it was going to be the last.

The taste of copper filled my mouth.

I straightened, touching a finger to my lip and

surveying the blood that dripped from it. My father didn't budge.

"You've always despised me," I said as I lifted my chin to face him once more. The man standing in front of me, sloppy and drunk and barely alive, was a stranger to me. He was nothing. He was certainly no father. "I'm not surprised at all that you made this deal to save your own skin. Just do yourself a favor and leave Tessa alone when I'm gone. It's the least you could do after ruining my life."

I didn't wait for him to respond. He grunted something behind me, but I ignored him and continued to my room, shutting the door firmly behind me.

Anger pounded through my ears. I rested my forehead on the wooden door and tried to breathe.

"We won't survive without you, Jade," Tessa whispered from our bed. Her and I shared a room in our small, broken-down cottage. I didn't mind it most nights, especially when my father was as temperamental and uncontrollable as he was. I could keep her safe this way.

"You will," I said to her. "You will survive because you have no choice. He won't help you, so you have to do this yourself." I walked to the bed and ripped off my old, torn boots. I supposed I wouldn't be needing them anymore, anyway. "You have food. Save as much money as possible. As soon as you're old enough, you marry one of the nice boys in town and he'll take care of you. Do you understand?" I asked. My voice was harsh, but I didn't care. Tessa had been coddled her entire life, even in this cursed town.

She was about to face a fierce reality.

She nodded, eyes red from tears.

"Good," I said. It was the last thing I said to her for the rest of the night. She curled into the bed beside me, sniffling silently as she drifted off to sleep. I stayed awake, however. Thinking about all of the things I would have rather done on my last day alive.

Pounding on the front door jolted me from my restless sleep.

"Go away!" my father yelled in a sluggish, half-awaken voice from somewhere within the house.

My body was already buzzing with energy. I knew exactly who was pounding at the door.

It was the fae prince's help coming to collect his human bride.

"Jade Farrow," a young man yelled. "We're here to take you to the compound."

The compound. The magnificent fae palace sounded more like a prison confinement.

I was already sitting up and pulling on the same torn up boots I wore every day.

"No," Tessa stirred awake next to me. "No, not yet! It's too early! I thought we would have the morning!"

I looked at her and placed a hand on each of her shoulders. "You have to be strong now, Tessa. Your future is up to you now. Do you understand?" She nodded silently. "Good. You know what to do. I'll survive, you know I will." A lie. "I'll write to you as soon as I can, okay? And if I'm allowed to come back for you, I will. I'll find a way to keep you safe Tessa, but you have to hang on until then. Can you do that?"

Tears welled in her giant, childish eyes. "Don't cry," I said sternly before I pulled her into a quick, tight hug. "Don't cry."

"I love you," she whispered into my shoulder.

Now it was my turn to blink away tears. "I love you too, bug."

"Jade Farrow!" The voice from the door yelled again.

"Coming!" I yelled back, the small slither of peace from hugging Tessa now gone. I stood up, not bothering for a change of clothes, and walked to the front door. I didn't look for my father. I didn't look back at my sister. They were on their own now, and so was I.

My hand froze on the doorknob, just for a moment. This was it. This was the moment my entire life's downfall began. From this moment forward, I was no longer in control. The guards would take me to the fae lands, and I would never be coming back.

It had been a long seventeen years. Life had been a stubborn bitch, I'd have to give her that.

Before I could cry, I swung the door open.

"You really can't let a woman sleep in on her wedding day?" I sneered, taking in the four guards that stood at my door.

No wings. No sparkling skin, no magical powers. They were human. That was a surprise.

"Apologies, miss," the younger man responded, hand over his chest. He couldn't have been more than a few years older than myself. "His Majesty likes to follow a strict schedule. We wouldn't want to be late."

"No," I huffed, shoving past him and stepping toward the carriage that was bound to be the gossip of the entire village for the next decade. "We certainly wouldn't want that."

One of the guards opened the small, golden door to the carriage. It was quite a show, that was certain. I grabbed his hand, about to step inside when my father stumbled out the door behind me.

"Stop!" He yelled, more coherent than I had ever seen him. His voice cracked as he continued, "Stop! That is my daughter! You can't take her!"

"Father–" I started.

The young guard stepped in front of him, blocking his path to me. "You wish to go back on the deal you made with His Majesty?" He spoke.

My father froze.

No, I thought. He can't go back on his deal. That would mean death for him, and he was much too selfish to ever do something like that.

But then my father looked at me, a look of pure helplessness strung across his tired features. "Jade," he mouthed.

"I'll be okay," I said with a straight face. "Take care of Tessa."

Tessa chose that moment to exit the house, grabbing my father's arm.

"No!" My father yelled again, anger flooding through the air. "Jade, don't go! Please! I'm so sorry. I'm so sorry, I'm so sorry, I'm so sorry," he was babbling now, lowering himself to his knees in a plea. Tessa was the one to comfort him this time.

Tears were streaming down my father's face. I never expected this from him. From the day he informed me about the deal he made with the fae king, I was certain he never cared about me.

Apparently, I had been wrong.

I turned my back on my family anyway, stepping into the golden carriage. I didn't look back. Not as the rest of the guards mounted their horses. Not as the carriage jolted into motion. And not as my father screamed for me to come back.

It wasn't until we were miles away from my house, from everything I ever loved, and from everything I was being ripped away from that I let the first tear fall. I didn't care that the guard across from me in the carriage saw. I didn't care if he thought I was weak or foolish. I was walking into my death. I didn't really care about anything anymore.

"Your family loves you very much," the man across from me said.

I scoffed. "Don't pretend you know anything about my life. And we don't have to play nice, either."

He straightened. "You are going to be the new bride

to the prince. The least I can do is make your acquaintance, Lady Farrow."

"The prince," I repeated, playing with the name on the end of my tongue. "So tell me..."

"Serefin."

"Tell me, Serefin, are the rumors true? Will I be dying today?"

He paused. "Don't believe everything you hear, Lady Farrow. The Royal Family is very complicated. Your prince in particular. I think you'll find much of what you've heard about the fae to be just that. Rumors."

I considered his words.

"How did you come to work for them?" I asked Serefin. "How did you enter the fae lands?"

A wicked smile crossed his face. "You believe me to be human, Lady Farrow?"

My heart pounded in my chest. It was impossible. He looked exactly like a human. There was nothing strange about him. Nothing peculiar. Nothing *fae*.

"You're fae?" I asked, not able to keep the shock out of my voice.

Serefin nodded.

"But you look..."

"Glamour," he replied. "His Majesty did not want to frighten you on your wedding day. He suggested we use glamour to keep our appearances...human-like."

"He doesn't want to scare me, huh?" I continued. "Very hypocritical coming from a man who is rumored to kill all of his human wives."

"You'll be safe, Jade," Serefin said, losing his calm and collected composure. "Your husband...well, let's just say that he doesn't like it when people touch his things. You will be safe. Please do not worry yourself with believing anything other than that."

A certain edge to his voice caused me to reconsider any argument I might have had. I had no idea what I was walking into, and the things Serefin said were not helping that situation.

My husband, one of the cruel and ruthless fae Princes of Rewyth, was going to protect me?

I nearly laughed out loud.

"I hate to do this, Lady Farrow, but His Majesty insists that you are asleep for the trip to Rewyth. Would you mind?" he asked politely, handing me a small vile of liquid.

"Is this going to kill me?" I asked skeptically.

Serefin laughed. "I sure hope not. A lot of people are looking forward to this wedding of yours."

I closed my eyes and dumped the vile of liquid into my mouth, swallowing it all. "It wouldn't be the worst thing in the world if it did though, would it?" I asked him, passing the empty vile back. "If it killed me?" I didn't care if I sounded weak or pitiful. I was dreading whatever came next. To die in my sleep would be merciful compared to what was going to happen next.

It might have been the sudden sluggishness I felt in my senses, but I could have sworn I saw his brows furrowed in concern as my own eyes drifted shut, the sound of the horse's hooves pounding repeatedly on the ground lulling me back to sleep.

I was in a bed when I woke up. Correction, I was in the biggest damn bed I had ever seen in my entire life.

"Oh good!" A woman, not much older than me, sat in a chair opposite of the bed. "You're awake! Good thing, because we have a lot of work to do. No offense, of course."

"Where are we?" I asked, rubbing my pounding temple. "How long was I out?"

"Just a couple of hours. The wedding starts soon, though, so up up!" she chirped, clapping her hands and pulling the blanket away from my body. "I'm Adeline, by the way. It's a pleasure to meet you."

I shook the small hand she held out for me. Adeline was beautiful, perhaps the most beautiful woman I had ever seen. She had bright red hair that cascaded in perfect curls to her waist, contrasting against her porcelain white skin.

"You're..."

"Fae, yes," she said, already knowing my question. "I'm also your soon-to-be sister-in-law. I insisted on helping you get ready today, mostly because these maids have no sense of style. But also because you and I are going to be best friends!"

I smiled as best I could to be polite, but this was all

too much. Adeline was fae, too? So far, none of the fae I had met were monstrous, evil creatures. Serefin and Adeline were both kind to me. Unless of course this was all a facade.

"I'm marrying your brother?" I asked as she pulled me into the bathroom. "Please tell me everything I've heard about the fae princes isn't true."

Adeline didn't even try to hide the pity she felt for me. "Sweetie, there's a lot to learn about my brothers. If I told you everything, we would be here for weeks on end. But I'll tell you this much," she said, guiding me to a chair and sitting me in front of a large mirror. "My brother isn't everything he seems on the surface. Give him a chance. He really might surprise you."

"Great," I mumbled. "I can't wait."

She grabbed a brush and picked up my long, black hair, running it through her fingers. "He'll love this too, you know."

I scoffed. "No offense, but I hardly care about whether or not my new captor likes the way I look."

"Captor?" she repeated. "Rewyth has to be a step up from the human lands at least, no?"

I shook my head slowly, fighting the sudden urge to cry. "I left my sister behind. She'll die without me. She'll starve."

"My brother will take care of your family. The fae aren't as cruel as the humans might have told you, you know."

She spoke matter-of-factly, but I wasn't entirely

sure I could trust her. I wasn't sure I could trust any of them.

"Well one good thing about Rewyth is the drinks, so please drink up. We both know you're going to need it," she chirped, passing me a crystal glass of clear, bubbly liquid. I had never been into drinking, mostly because of my father. But today, I would be an idiot to object. "Here's a piece of advice, though," she continued. "This is the same liquor you have in the human lands, but don't drink anything else tonight. The fae have special drinks that will be way too...powerful for you. So, stick to this stuff."

"Thank you," I said to her, noting her warning. "Really, thank you for being nice to me."

"Of course, darling. You've been through enough already. Now let's make you beautiful. It is your day, after all," she winked and tapped her glass against mine. I took a small sip of my drink. The liquid was sweet and light. It burned in my stomach, but it was better than the ball of nerves I had been trying to ignore.

Adeline worked through my hair for what felt like hours before moving to my face. Her touch was gentle, which I was grateful for. She didn't ask me about the scars on my back or the recent bruise on my face, although her hands worked extra carefully when she addressed those areas. She spoke to me about the traditions of weddings in Rewyth, and about everything I should be expecting today.

She didn't mention the fact that I might die. I didn't ask.

Hours later, I stared at myself in the mirror. I hardly recognized myself. Adeline was definitely magic, after all. My hair looked just as perfect as hers, jet black instead of her fiery red. My skin was spotless. I was still pale, but she had covered every flaw. Hidden every scar. I looked...pretty.

And my dress was more magnificent than anything I could have imagined. It was pure gold, not white like I had expected. The silk fabric hung to my thin curves, a tight corset giving me a figure I never knew existed. I had to admit, with the exposed back and the low neckline, I was showing more skin than I ever had in my life. But as Adeline had said, the fae world was different. She had actually called this dress *modest*.

"One last touch," she said, walking toward me with a white gift box. "This is for you. From your future husband."

My stomach sank. "How generous," I mocked, lifting the lid to the box. My jaw nearly dropped when I saw what was inside.

It was a knife. A black, perfectly welded steel knife with a delicate, artistic handle.

Emotion rumbled in my chest.

"You like it?" Adeline asked.

"It's perfect. Absolutely perfect."

And I meant that. I didn't realize how exposed I would feel without the knife I had lost with the wolves last night. This was a massive upgrade.

"Well, I suppose I can't send you to the vipers

without some form of protection. Just promise me you won't use it on me!" she joked.

I laughed with her and hiked up my dress. Adeline helped me strap it to the inside of my thigh. As if a simple blade would protect me from the fae.

I took a deep, shaky breath.

"You ready?" she chirped. "I'm sure everyone is dying to meet you!"

I smiled and nodded. "Am I allowed to say no?"

She laughed and hooked her arm through mine. "You'll be fine," she insisted. "But a piece of sisterly advice? Don't trust the other brothers. I love my family, but the boys have minds of their own. Especially when it comes to wives."

That last part I knew.

"Serefin said the prince would keep me safe. Is that true?" I asked.

She thought for a moment before answering. "If my brother is around, you'll be the safest human in the kingdom."

I let go of a breath I was holding. Adeline seemed genuine enough. If she was warning me against the other princes, at least she wasn't entirely full of shit.

"Can I ask something of you, Adeline?"

"Of course you can, honey. What is it?"

"If this goes badly...if I die today...will you take care of my sister? My family, I mean. They need food, they need money, they–"

"Yes, Jade. Of course, I will. You mustn't worry

about it anymore, okay? You have my word. Besides, everything will go perfectly."

I blinked once. "I hope you're right."

We walked through the massive stone hallways, our heels clicking the porcelain floors in dreadful unison.

I tried not to stare at the pure magnificence of the compound. The walls, which were so tall I had to bend my neck to view the top, were covered in artistically crafted black molding and green vines. Every detail was created with perfection. The vines weaved across the walls as we walked, arching around every massive window that let in a perfect amount of sunlight.

It was beautiful.

Beautifully horrific, I reminded myself. These walls were my jail cell, as gorgeous as they may be. This compound was no haven. It was filled with evil and torture and malice. It housed the worst family in the entire kingdom.

These beautiful details were no more than a facade.

Adeline walked me to a pair of massive black doors. My future husband and the rest of the fae were on the other side, I could feel it in my bones. I took a deep breath and rolled my shoulders back. If the Prince of Rewyth thought he was going to get another ignorant human wife who would kneel before him and thank him for killing her, he was terribly wrong.

I wasn't going out that easily.

The massive doors swung open.

"You'll be fine," Adeline whispered to me. "I'll find you after the ceremony."

I nodded at her, but I was frozen where I stood. Hundreds of people filled the ballroom, everyone now staring directly at me.

I forced myself not to shiver, now very aware of how much skin was showing.

I kept my eyes on the floor directly in front of me. The room was silent. I was certain everyone could hear how fast my heart was pounding. Fae could hear that stuff, right?

It didn't matter. *Keep moving forward*, I told myself. *Move forward and stay alive.*

I walked down the aisle, gold dress flowing behind me, until I arrived at the front.

"Well come up here, girl, we don't have all day," one of the men at the altar said. I had to look. I had to lift my head and lay eyes on the fae prince that was going to ruin my life.

"Jade," a softer, familiar voice said. This caused me to finally lift my eyes. *I had heard that voice before.*

When I met his eyes, I nearly vomited.

Standing in front of me, waiting for me to arrive at the end of the aisle, was Mal.

No. Not Mal. The Prince of Rewyth. The Prince of Shadows.

My soon to be husband.

CHAPTER 3
Jade

The King and Queen sat on a pair of thrones next to us. This was a guess, but considering the golden crowns they wore, I assumed it was a pretty good guess.

"Prince Malachi," the king growled from his throne, "Please take your beloved by both hands."

My heart was racing. Mal was Prince Malachi? Mal–Prince Malachi–was fae?

Not just any fae. A fae prince. *My* fae prince. The Prince of Shadows.

"Don't worry," Malachi whispered with a smile, clearly noticing my hesitation. "It will be over soon."

Over soon? Was he talking about the ceremony, or my life?

He held his hands out, inviting me to take them. If I declined, they would certainly kill me on the spot.

The way the King was looking at me confirmed it.

Like he was waiting for me to make a mistake so he could end my useless, human life.

I took Malachi's hands.

They weren't as cold as I had expected. They were large and warm, and he held my hands gently, as if he wanted to give me some space.

I tried to keep my hands still but couldn't stop the mild shaking.

His respect was a facade. I knew enough to know that the fae, however kind they may seem on the surface, were creatures of malice.

Especially the Prince of Shadows.

"Jade Farrow," The King said, standing from his throne and approaching us. Malachi's hands tightened around mine, just barely. His shoulders stiffened as his father approached. "Let me be the first one to formally welcome you to Rewyth. As I'm sure you've heard, these lands are precious to us. Generations of fae have lived and died to protect the very ground you stand on today."

I held back an eye roll. If he really intended to preach to me on how noble the fae of Rewyth were, he could hold his breath. I knew better than to listen to any of them.

"You are not the first human to enter the compound, and likely will not be the last," he continued. "Yet my son remains in need of a wife. A human wife, who will bring together our lands and create peace across all of Rewyth. Your duty here is not just that of Prince Malachi's wife, but as a leader to our people."

One of the men standing behind Malachi, his brother I assumed, laughed. I turned my attention to the brothers. They looked nothing like Malachi. Malachi was tall and sculpted, with dark hair and brooding shoulders. His brothers were lighter, in both color and muscle. They looked young, and based on their inappropriate laughter, I assumed they were just as immature as they looked.

"Prince Malachi," the King said, turning my attention back to him. "Jade Farrow stands here to become your wife. It is your duty to protect her with your life. It is your duty to honor her as you would your own, and it is your duty to fulfill these vows as long as you both live."

More laughter erupted from behind us. Heat flushed my cheeks.

The King continued.

"Do you agree to uplift these vows for the future of Rewyth?" he asked.

"Yes," Malachi responded without a second of hesitation.

The King turned to me. His eyes were an electric blue, almost shocking to look at. But there was something cold in his gaze. Something... *fae.*

A chill ran down my spine.

"Lady Farrow," he addressed me. "As wife to Prince Malachi and princess of Rewyth, it is your duty to honor and protect Prince Malachi, it is your duty to honor this wedding agreement and it is your duty to lead our people as you would your own for as long as you both live."

My heart was pounding in my chest.

This was all happening too fast.

"Do you agree to uplift these vows?"

I looked away from the King and back to Mal. Back to *Prince Malachi*. My soon to be husband.

He was shockingly handsome. That much I could not deny. But his gaze was harsh and evil. He had seen and done terrible things. He would do terrible things again, he would likely do terrible things to me.

But I had made it all the way here. I had to do this for Tessa, I reminded myself.

And frankly, I had no choice. Any one of these fae could kill me in a heartbeat.

I blushed when I realized I had been staring, but I did not look away. He smirked as if he knew what I was thinking. I was not going to show him weakness. He wanted a scared, submissive human that would bow down at anything these fae said.

I was not going to be that wife. I was not going to be that human.

"Yes," I said strongly. Malachi looked almost... shocked.

I didn't move a muscle. I kept my chin high, even as the brothers continued to giggle and snicker. I saw the way they stared at the exposed skin on my body, yet I did not move to cover it.

I was not going to die as a weak little girl.

"Excellent," the King said, pulling a small knife and grabbing Malachi's closest hand from mine. The King roughly sliced Malachi's skin, blood pooling in his palm. He grabbed my hand, skin cold as ice, and did the same. Despite my best effort, I flinched as the pain stung my hand. The blood pooled in my palm, and the King clasped both of our hands together. The blood flowed together, down our fingertips and onto the floor.

"Jade Farrow, Princess, welcome to Rewyth," the King said. Before I could object, he grabbed my face with both hands and planted a harsh, nasty kiss onto my cheek.

I was frozen. Vile rose in my throat. If this was any type of wedding tradition that the fae followed, I was not a fan. Especially when his wandering hands found the skin on my bare back.

Just before panic began to set in, Malachi grabbed my shoulders and pulled me backward, away from the King's grasp. I opened my mouth to object to whatever the Saints had just happened, but Malachi squeezed my shoulder. A warning.

"You must learn to share, father," Malachi said. This elicited more laughter from the brothers, but something dark and hateful laced each of his words. I dared a glance at the queen, who sat silently with a bored look on her face.

The King laughed. "You can't blame a man for noticing beauty," he said. "And you should be thanking me for finding you such a stunning human this time."

This time.

"Now, Prince Malachi," he said, gathering his composure once more. "Kiss your wife, and let the party begin!"

I could still feel the King's lips on my skin. I couldn't do it again. I couldn't let them defile me this way.

But Prince Malachi was my husband now. This kiss was going to be the least of my worries. Malachi stepped forward, coming just inches from my face. I prepared myself for the worst, but felt relieved when he simply placed a quick, featherlight kiss on my lips.

I supposed it was better than the King's kiss, but I could still feel my cheeks flushing pink.

Cheers of applause erupted in the room. I had completely forgotten about the hundreds of fae witnessing the ceremony. Certainly, they were all here for the food and booze the fae were rumored to indulge in.

Malachi placed a hand on my lower back. "Stay by my side," he whispered close to my ear, loud enough for only me to hear. I gave him a small nod of acknowledgement and let him guide me back down the aisle I had just come from.

Except now, I was not just a human girl in the fae world.

I was the wife to Rewyth's Prince of Shadows.

Had the other wives survived this long? Or was this when they all were killed?

It didn't matter. There was nothing I could do here with hundreds of fae surrounding me. I held my chin high and kept a straight, emotionless face as Malachi led us through the crowd and out the giant doors. As the large doors were closing, I heard the King make a muffled announcement, which cued a loud chorus of music and even more cheers from the crowd.

The doors boomed shut behind us.

We were alone in the hallway.

He dropped his hand from my back and paced to the large window near us, running his hands through his dark hair.

I assessed the situation.

The knife was still strapped to my thigh. If I aimed perfectly, I had a chance at stabbing his heart.

But would it kill him?

I doubted it. And it wasn't worth the risk. I had to survive the night, and then I would make my escape.

But what of Tessa? Our deal would be broken if I ran away. She could starve if I didn't make it home alive.

No. There was only one way to survive this. And it was to be the damned human Princess of Rewyth.

"Mal," I said, breaking the silence. He spun around to face me, leaning against the window ledge. *Do not be afraid,* I told myself. "You came to see me yesterday. Why? Why didn't you tell me who you were?"

His eyes scanned my body, pausing at the busted lip Adeline had poorly attempted to conceal. "What happened?" he asked. The fierceness in his voice almost made me step back. I fought the urge to cover my lip.

"Nothing," I said, touching a finger to the painful

area. I wasn't about to unload what happened with my father last night. I had larger issues here.

His eyes squinted like he was about to call me out for the lie. I spoke before he had the chance and asked, "Answer my question. Why were you in the forest yesterday? Fae aren't supposed to be in the human lands."

His eyes scanned my body once before meeting my own. "I am not allowed to see my wife before I marry her?"

Heat creeped up my neck at the way he stared at me.

"I assumed you wouldn't care much either way," I said. I hated how weak it sounded, but I stood my ground anyway. If I was going to die tonight, I wanted to dig up as much information as possible. "Your wives have never lived that long anyway, right? How long until you tire of me, too?"

His eyes grew dark and he pushed himself off the window ledge, coming so close I could feel his breath on my cheek. It was the same dominance I saw from him in the forest yesterday against the wolves.

"Let me get one thing straight here, *princess*. My other wives have been killed, yes, but not by me."

My eyes widened.

"Shocked?" He asked. *Yes.* "Surprised that the deadly, feral Prince of Shadows is not killing each of his wives after they are wed?" a low, evil laugh rumbled in his chest. "You have a lot to learn, Jade. And we're about to spend the evening with hundreds of drunk, idiotic fae who haven't seen a human in decades."

If he was trying to scare me, it was working.

"So do yourself a favor and stay by my side. Don't trust any of them, and hold onto that little toy strapped to your leg," he said, eyes flickering down my dress once more. "You're not safe here, princess. But I'm not losing another wife. I don't care how many fae assholes it costs me."

He stopped talking but didn't back away. I stood there, staring into his dark, passionate eyes. "That's good to know," I admitted after a few awkward seconds. I couldn't believe he was talking about the other fae—his family—this way. From what I could tell, he despised them. Especially his brothers.

Malachi broke our gaze first, walking back to the massive doors of the ballroom. When he held his hand out to me, I took it. "A bit of advice," he said, "don't drink anything."

I didn't have time to ask for an explanation. Malachi pushed the large doors open once more, and we were greeted with the same group of fae.

Except things had certainly gotten rowdy in the few minutes we were out of the room.

Music flowed through the massive ballroom, echoing off the stone walls. The reserved audience from earlier was now standing, dancing, and drinking away. Never-ending tables of food lined the perimeter of the room, and servants walked around with trays of drinks for every guest.

Malachi navigated us through the crowd. The others had a large level of respect for him, bowing their heads as he passed. Part of me wondered if they were just as afraid of him as the humans were.

What had he done to get his reputation? How many people had he killed? Tortured? Tormented?

I shook my head. None of that mattered now. What mattered was getting out of here alive, and Malachi was my best chance at that.

I squeezed his hand tighter, hoping he didn't realize how nervous I was. I was the only human in this entire room, perhaps even this entire compound.

I was going to find out just how much fae hated humans, after all.

CHAPTER 4
Malachi

I knew two things to be true:

One. Someone was attempting to murder Jade tonight.

Two. I was going to rip the head off anyone who tried.

I knew both of those two things to be true the first time I laid eyes on her.

Besides, I was sick of people *touching my things.*

We just had to make it through this party. And then I could protect her. But here, with hundreds of fae around us...

It would be nearly impossible.

There were dozens of reasons for numerous different people to want her dead.

Correction–they wanted *me* to be an unmarried, desperate, brooding bastard. They didn't give a damn about whether Jade lived or died. I didn't trust a single one of those snakes.

Jade's grip on my hand tightened as we walked through the sea of drunk, dancing guests. She had never seen fae before. Not that she realized, anyway. Surely this was overwhelming for her.

I don't know why I cared. I *didn't* care. But we were going to survive the night. *That* is what I cared about.

Not her. I wasn't stupid enough to let myself care about a human.

Not again. *Never* again.

I pulled her toward the front of the room, nodding at my brothers who sat at the end of the massive stone table.

And no–I didn't trust them either.

But they knew better than to even look in our direction as Jade sat down awkwardly in the seat beside me.

Her eyes were massive, darting around the room at every movement. Her face was stone, but those eyes gave everything away. She may not have been afraid, but she was alert.

Good girl.

I let go of her hand but draped my arm around the back of her chair. "As soon as everyone's drunk, we can leave," I whispered to her. "Shouldn't take long."

She stiffened, and I knew it was at the feel of my breath against her ear.

Jade hated me. Like all humans, she hated fae, and anyone who had to do with the fae. She likely hated me

45

even more because she recognized me as the man from the forest last night.

But I couldn't tell her why I had come to see her in the forest.

Especially with all the annoyingly large, fae ears lingering around.

"Your fourth wedding," Lucien, one of my brothers, announced from the end of the table. A certain stillness filled the air, but I could tell by the boldness alone that Lucien was drunk.

Absolutely plastered.

"You're a lucky man," he continued, "to have not one, not two, not even three... but four parties thrown in your favor. Truly, what an honor, Prince of Shadows."

"Watch it," I growled casually. Lucien's only warning, and he knew it.

The other brothers' relationship didn't bother me. When I was younger, I had been jealous. Of course, I had been. But I was stupid and arrogant back then.

I didn't understand why they hated me. I didn't understand why they were desperate to get ahead every step of the way.

But now, I understood. After learning that I was the one and only true heir to the fae throne, I understood.

My mother had been the true Queen to Rewyth. She still was. But after my father remarried and had four sons, things got complicated.

They would never stand a chance. All four of them.

So, they hated me for it. For decades, they had taunted me and envied me. But I never really cared. Not after those first initial years, after I had learned what type of people they really were.

What type of men they really were.

I was never going to be anything like them, and they hated me because of it.

"What?" I blinked at Jade, realizing she had asked me a question.

"Are you going to eat?" she repeated, clearly pleased by my level of distraction.

"You're hungry?" I asked. *Idiot.* She was obviously starving, likely hadn't eaten a single thing since we dragged her from her home, and I had dragged her in here through the crowd of food without offering her anything.

She had been starving herself so her sister could have food. I *knew* that. I had seen it firsthand.

"Stay here," I admitted, forcing down the wave of anger that rushed forward at the single thought of Jade providing for her ungrateful family. "I'll grab you some food. Don't move."

She nodded in acceptance. I did my best not to stare at the exposed skin on her chest as I stood from the chair and walked toward the crowd of guests.

It didn't take more than a few seconds before Kara approached me in the sea, wrapping her skinny arm around my own.

"If you want a real party," she purred, flicking her

tongue across her red lipstick, "you know where I'll be."

"Not tonight, Kara," I insisted. "I'm a married man. That's over." *However long that would last.*

The disappointment on her face didn't go unnoticed, but I couldn't bring myself to give a shit. I had told Kara many times that I wasn't interested.

But I guess I couldn't blame her for trying.

I wasn't that person anymore. There was a time when I would have jumped at any chance to get absolutely trashed with the other fae and slept with someone like Kara, but not anymore.

I had a duty to uphold. A vow to keep.

Kara shook her head but didn't remove her hand from my arm. "I mean it," I warned. "That's enough."

"You know you'll grow tired of her," she muttered. "I can keep you happy, Malachi. I can—"

I snapped, taking her hand off my arm and gripping so hard I knew it hurt her. I let my power rumble, just enough for her to sense it was there. "Don't make me repeat myself. This is already embarrassing enough for you. Now get your things and go."

Her brows furrowed before she snatched her hand from mine. She mumbled something under her breath and stalked away. I didn't bother even giving her a second glance.

Kara was nice. Sometimes. But even if I wasn't destined to marry a human, things would have never worked out with her. Kara was a spitting image of what the humans hated so much when it came to the fae. Kara was selfish, materialistic, ignorant, and naive.

Still. I couldn't help but wonder if it was her own fault, or this warped reality we had been living for the past few decades. We sat in this castle pretending nothing else existed outside of it.

Like I said. Ignorant.

I brought my attention back to the food I was searching for.

My father–the king–was standing just a few feet away. I could have turned around, tried to avoid him, but that would no doubt result in some sort of punishment later.

And right now, I needed him on my side.

Especially if Jade Farrow was going to survive the night.

"Thank you for all of this," I said, throwing the *grateful son* smile on my face as I approached my father. "It's a beautiful party."

His companions nodded and found themselves busy with other conversation as I approached.

"It's not every day that your firstborn son gets married! Although, it might be every few years. Perhaps we should keep the decor for next time, yes?"

It was a joke, but my temper flared. I clenched my fists, trying to keep my cool.

"Relax, son. Your wife seems to be a fighter. No doubt this one will be different!" Every word was a lie. "Besides...fourth time's the charm, right?" he said, stumbling over his words and sloshing the liquid from his cup as he leaned toward me.

"You're drunk already?" I asked. "With so much of the night left ahead?"

He took another drink. "It's a party, boy. You should enjoy it while you can."

"Not much to enjoy when my wife is in danger," I admitted through gritted teeth.

My father's face grew serious. "You're married not even an hour and she already has you running around for her own protection!" he laughed. "You really don't think you can trust this room full of your closest friends and family?" he asked.

I looked around the room. Strangers. That's who these people were to me. They weren't friends, and they certainly weren't family.

"I thought I could trust them the last three times, and look where that got us."

My father's eyes darkened. "Your wife is safe, Malachi. Don't be a fool. Not a single person in this room wishes harm on her."

A small slice of anger laced his words. Was he really pissed that I didn't trust this room full of drunk, selfish fae? Or was he more pissed off because I was actually taking a stance and protecting my wife?

I wanted nothing more than to stand up to him. My power was no match for his, and we both knew that.

But my father had leverage. That one piece of information that forced me to obey his every command, his every wish.

I held his gaze until I heard Jade's laugh echo in the room behind me.

"Excuse me, *my wife* is waiting," I mumbled to my father before turning around, *without* any food, and returning to the table.

One glimpse of my brother's white hair and I knew exactly what had made Jade so cheerful. My brother Lucien had moved his chair a few feet closer to Jade's, separating himself from the others and leaning in to fill her ear with nothing but nonsense, I was sure.

Jade's demeanor had flipped entirely since I had walked away. She sat at the table with both elbows propping her head up, tossing her chin back and laughing at something Lucien was saying.

Lucien. Certainly the least trustworthy of my brothers. But Jade didn't know that. And Lucien was clever enough to ensure she thought the exact opposite.

"I leave for two minutes and you start having fun without me?" I chirped, sliding back into my seat.

Jade hardly glanced in my direction, her long black hair spilling over her shoulder.

"Your brother here was just filling me in on exactly what type of family I've married myself into," Jade said with a smile still plastered on her face.

"Is that so?" I asked.

Lucien nodded, his dark eyes drinking up every second of her attention. "Nothing too terrible yet, brother. We must ease her into these types of things. But I did inform your beautiful bride here that of all the idiot Rewyth princes, you may be the only one who has managed to set the castle on fire." A wicked grin played on his lips.

I pretended to be amused by the memory, but I knew what Lucien was doing.

He was trying to piss me off.

We both knew that I wasn't the one who set the castle on fire. I was just the one who got blamed.

Like I got blamed for everything else growing up.

Lucien leaned in to whisper into Jade's ear again, now just inches from Jade's face. His eyes flickered over every one of her features.

I draped my arm across Jade's shoulders, squeezing lightly. A clear display to my brothers, to Lucien, to back off.

"I'm sure Jade's heard enough," I interjected, trying my best to sound as bored as possible. Jade whipped her head to me.

"He was just telling me–"

"I said *enough*!" I boomed. I didn't care that the words came out too strong. I didn't care that she flinched at my voice.

Lucien needed to learn. And frankly, so did Jade.

Lucien held my gaze a second longer before he sat up and returned to his original position at the table.

I didn't take my arm off Jade's shoulders, but did my best to touch as little of her as possible. As if that would help. Any type of relaxation she was displaying just seconds ago was gone now, replaced by the strong look of a woman who wanted to survive.

The thought of Lucien getting so close to Jade with that look on his face made me want to throw him across the ballroom.

But then people would think I cared. Which I didn't.

I had expected the snakes to come out of the swamp at this wedding. I should have expected my brothers to be four of them.

And like I said. I was tired of people touching my things.

CHAPTER 5
Jade

"What a beautiful bride!" Adeline said as she approached our table that was apparently reserved for family...and myself.

"Thank you, Adeline," I said. "Although a bit more fabric would have been nice."

"Malachi, she is simply gorgeous," Adeline continued. Malachi looked at me sideways and raised an eyebrow.

"Yes," he said, causing me to fight a blush. "She is, isn't she?"

I was shocked that he would admit a compliment so easily. But I was his wife, after all. I supposed it wasn't the worst thing in the world if he agreed that I wasn't hideous.

Not like I cared.

Malachi relaxed back into his chair, sprawling his legs in front of him in a nonchalant demeanor. His arm still rested across my shoulders. A predator staking claim on his prey.

A shiver shuttered through me.

The rest of the princes, Malachi's brothers, busied themselves with whispering and giggling, no doubt talking about their *new sister*.

They stole glances at Malachi every few seconds, but he didn't seem to spend a single second thinking about any of them. After my conversation with Lucien, I was skeptical. Although he seemed friendly enough, Malachi didn't trust him. I could tell by the way he sat next to me, tense and tracking every movement his brother made.

Malachi didn't even trust his family around me. *Noted.*

"Everyone is here?" Malachi asked Adeline in a low voice as she took a seat at the table.

She nodded. "Including the King of Paseocan."

A low growl escaped Malachi's throat at the name. I tuned in, suddenly interested in whatever quarrel they may have that would make Malachi react this way to him.

The killer of his past wives, perhaps?

If there was one thing I would listen to Malachi about, it was not to trust anyone. Not a single one of these wicked fae were off my list, which meant my guard was up.

Even if I had to pretend to be the stupid human who would laugh at any of their jokes.

Malachi shifted in his seat, and his leg brushed mine. If he noticed, he didn't seem to care. Or react.

He whispered something to Adeline, most likely about the King of Paseocan they had mentioned, and her eyes glanced over me once before she stood from the table and lost herself in the sea of guests.

"Something wrong?" I asked, hiding my nerves with strong words.

"Nothing you need to worry about," he said. Spoken like a true asshole, assuming I am too dumb to know anything of value.

But I bit my tongue.

Malachi moved to whisper in my ear, coming so close that his lips nearly brushed my skin. "What did I tell you about my brothers?" he asked.

I didn't back away as I turned my head slightly and replied, "I don't take orders from you, *prince*." If Malachi were to move an inch, his forehead would be touching mine. But he stilled where he was, challenging me with the darkness in his eyes, before finally leaning back in his chair once more.

This action alone drew dozens of eyes our direction, including a few looks of jealousy from a couple different women around the room.

Impressive.

I didn't miss the way he interacted with the beautiful blonde fae as he was walking around the room earlier. But Malachi was the most powerful prince in Rewyth. Surely, he had women throwing themselves at him for any chance at power.

And surely, he had taken them up on their offers from time to time.

I kept my gaze anywhere other than Malachi's brothers, especially Lucien, but I knew they could sense how nervous I was. I was sure they could hear every heartbeat. I was sure they could smell the sweat that glistened on my brow.

I was sure Malachi could, as well.

But my efforts of ignoring the brothers didn't last long.

"Care for a dance, *sister*," one of the princes said, rising from his chair and extending a pale hand in my direction.

I hesitated. After Malachi's warning, this was bold. But he didn't say a word, and everyone at the table locked their gaze onto me. It was a test, I was sure of it. The stupid human girl would be too terrified to dance with fae. Let alone a fae prince.

But like I said. I wasn't going to be that human. And my *husband* wasn't going to boss me around like I was his property.

"I must warn you," I said as I rose from my chair and took his hand. I could have sworn I heard Malachi growl once more, or maybe I had just imagined it. "I'm an awful dancer."

The rest of the brothers wore their shock on their faces. Even Lucien had a wicked grin of satisfaction from where he sat at the table. They were not expecting me to say yes.

"Then we must teach you the ways of the fae," the

prince said mischievously before leading me to the dance floor.

Tessa and I had learned to dance together, each of us taking turns on who was the boy and who was the girl. It had never come in handy for me, not until this moment. I was hoping, however, that Tessa could use the skills to seduce herself into a rich husband and get out of the burning pit that was our home.

She was always better than I was, I had to admit. But the fae prince–*not* my husband–tugged my body to his and led me into a long, graceful waltz.

"My name is Adonis, by the way," he whispered, each word tumbling off of his perfectly rounded lips. He was just as handsome as Malachi, each feature crafted with perfection. And he knew it.

"It's nice to officially meet you, Adonis," I replied. He turned us around the ballroom, and his grip tightened on my hip when I nearly lost my footing.

"Relax," he said. "I'm not going to hurt you."

I tensed in his grip. "What makes you think I am afraid of you?"

He smirked. "I am sure you have heard the rumors by now. Are you not curious as to who your enemies are in this very room?"

I looked over his shoulder, stealing a few glances at the wandering eyes that were practically gawking at us on the dance floor.

Gawking at me.

"I suppose I have been curious, yes. Although I haven't yet crossed any of you off the list."

"Smart girl," he purred.

Looks aside, he was nothing like Malachi. Lucien hadn't been, either. That much was obvious. All the princes had an annoying arrogance to them, but Adonis had something beneath his eyes that made my skin crawl. I was very aware of his cold skin touching my bare back.

I was also very aware of the knife that rested at my thigh.

"Why waste such a beautiful party if I am just going to be killed tonight, then?" I asked Adonis quietly.

He laughed under his breath. "My dear brother doesn't plan on his wives being killed, Lady Farrow. Besides, I think you might be his favorite," he said with a wink.

I scoffed. "Surely an entire ballroom full of capable, powerful fae would know who has assassinated not one, but three newlywed princesses." My words were bold but my nerves had finally settled. I was desperate for answers now.

I needed a plan.

The music changed, and Adonis pulled me closer to his chest as he transitioned into the next dance. I was close enough to feel his breath on my face, but I wasn't going to back away. They wanted me to be afraid. They wanted me to back down.

That sure as saints wasn't going to happen.

I lifted my chin to face him, finding nothing but amusement strung across his face.

"Am I wrong?" I urged.

"Careful, Lady Farrow," he whispered in my ear. "You're in a room full of men who won't like what you're implying."

"And what am I implying, exactly, Adonis?"

A flash of something crossed his face. Anger? Annoyance? But it quickly disappeared. "You want to look out for yourself, I understand that," he said. "It's respectable. Especially in a house full of fae. But every time Malachi is wed, his wife is assassinated. If we knew who was doing it, we would stop it. Malachi would stop it. I don't think he quite likes weddings enough to repeat them every few years, to be honest with you."

I glanced back to our table to find Malachi staring at us, watching our every move. Watching Adonis's every move.

I looked back to his brother. I didn't trust him, but he knew something. I could see it in his eyes.

"I like you, Lady Farrow," he continued. My eyes widened. "The other humans have been so...boring. And it's been a while since we've had some excitement in this castle. So, I'm going to help you."

My eyes nearly rolled out of my head. "How can you help me?"

"Three doors to the right from here, there's an unlocked room. Meet me there at midnight and I'll tell you everything I know."

My heart was pounding. Adonis kept tugging me across the dance floor. "But what about Malachi?"

Adonis glanced at his brother before returning his gaze to me. "I know you think you can trust him, but be very careful. You don't trust me," he said, "and that's a wise choice. You shouldn't. You shouldn't trust anyone in this room, Lady Farrow."

"You tell me not to trust you yet you expect me to mysteriously meet you at midnight?"

He smiled. "Someone is going to try to kill you tonight. I think it might be your only option."

If Adonis noticed the chill that ran down my back, he didn't show it. As he continued guiding me across the dance floor through the sea of people I couldn't trust, I began to realize the depth of the situation.

I couldn't trust a single person here. Not the person I was dancing with. Not Adeline, who had been so nice to me.

And not even my husband.

CHAPTER 6

Malachi

"It's not polite to stare," Adeline said. She bounced back toward the table and took Jade's empty seat next to me.

"I'm not staring, I'm observing," I corrected.

"Well, it's creepy. Adonis won't do anything to her, and you know that," she said in a low voice so only I could hear.

"I'm not too sure about that," I replied, mostly to myself. "Did you find anything?"

Adeline took a long drink from her glass and tossed a glance at my brothers, who were still lingering at the table.

She leaned toward me and whispered, "Just like you thought, Mal. Apparently our dearest father hand-picked each guard on duty tonight. The same guards will be guarding your rooms later tonight, also."

She didn't say anything else. She didn't have to.

Everything she was saying confirmed what I had been thinking all along.

My father was anticipating Jade's assassination just as much as I was. All that talk about being able to trust my family...what shit.

My father didn't trust them, either.

"It's going to be okay," Adeline said after a few moments. "We'll keep her safe. I don't care if I have to stay up all night."

I smiled. Adeline was one of the only people in this world I trusted with my life. With Jade's life, also.

Trust was a rare quality in Rewyth. Adeline had been by my side since we were kids. Except she didn't act any different when she learned that I was going to inherit the throne. Perhaps it was because as a female Fae, it was impossible for her to take the throne anyway. The others saw me as competition. Without me, Lucien would have the throne.

Since my title was announced, my brothers pushed me away. Although it didn't help that our father adores them all, yet finds me absolutely mortifying.

"I saw that little conversation you had with Kara," Adeline whispered. "What was that all about?"

I rolled my eyes. "Don't worry about it," I said.

"Well, I am worried about it. You have a wife, Malachi. You can't keep entertaining her like you're a bachelor in Rewyth."

"You know that's not what this is."

"Don't I?" she scoffed and leaned back in her seat.

"You're blind, brother. Always seeing people for their best qualities and ignoring the worst."

"I see who she is. Trust me, she's not an issue."

Adeline just shook her head. "You better be telling the truth. Jade's been through enough as it is. You don't need a jealous ex in the mix making things worse."

"I'm next!" One of the twins shouted, pointing to where Adonis and Jade still flowed through the dance floor.

This earned a roar of laughter from the others.

"You should get married more often, brother," Lucien announced. "It really brings some excitement to the family!"

"You're all pigs," Adeline sneered. "Jade is not a prize to be passed around, she's your new sister. And princess, might I add."

"Yeah? For how long?" Lucien retorted. I stood so fast my chair fell to the ground behind me.

I left them all at the table, Adeline yelling after me, as I stormed onto the dance floor to find my wife.

Jade stared at me with wide eyes as I approached.

"Do you mind?" I asked Adonis. He had always been the most mature of my brothers, and there had been times when I really wanted to trust him. I really wanted to believe he was different from the others.

But loyalty was expensive. And it wasn't a risk I was willing to take tonight.

Adonis gave a respectful nod and passed Jade's hand to mine. Unlike Lucien, Adonis would never disrespect me in front of everyone. In private, maybe, but not here.

Whatever walls Jade had dropped when she was dancing with Adonis were up again. Her face was blank and her posture was stiff, no doubt tracking each one of my movements as I took her small hand and led her slowly through the crowd of dancers.

"You seem to be getting along with my brothers," I said. She missed a small step, stumbling over my foot and nearly falling. I caught her around the waist as she fell into my chest. "And it also seems you were not lying about your dancing skills."

Jade huffed as she straightened. "No, *prince*, I was not lying. And your brothers have been...entertaining."

There was more to that, but I didn't push.

Although my curiosity was at an all-time high. Perhaps she needed more of a warning. Did she think I warned her from my brothers out of my own jealousy?

"Lucien is a hot head," I admitted. "He's relentless with women, and he'll pretty much say anything to get whatever he wants from you."

"And you think I'm the type to be easily manipulated by a few funny jokes or superficial compliments?"

Her jaw was sharp, matching her perfectly sculpted cheekbones. With her face this close to me, I could see every flash of emotion in her eyes. Even as she held a straight face.

Those eyes were daggers. Her sharpest weapon.

"I don't know," I said back. "I don't really know anything about you."

"Really? Stalking me in the forest didn't show you everything you needed to know?"

"Careful, princess," I whispered, very aware of the wandering ears around us. I tugged her closer to me, just an inch, and leaned down to her ear. "You don't want to give away all my secrets, do you?"

She tensed, but didn't back away. I continued talking.

"Adonis has always been my favorite brother. He's smart. He's respectful. But his loyalties are questionable."

"And what about you?" she asked. "Where do your loyalties lie?"

"My loyalties lie with myself, my future kingdom, and my wife," I said. The words came out harsh, but they were truthful. Jade had to know that. There were hundreds of rumors circling the human lands about me, I wasn't naive. But Jade had to know that she could trust me. She had to believe that I would do anything to protect her, and she had to believe that everything I did was for the future of my kingdom.

Everything.

Whoever was responsible for killing my wives wasn't going to get away with it again.

If the guards weren't going to catch whoever tried, I would do it myself.

"Your brothers don't seem to like you very much," she said. Her voice had softened, and she stepped close enough that her chest nearly touched my own as another song stopped and started again. Her hand moved from my shoulder to the base of my neck, taunting me.

Was she doing that on purpose?

I rolled my eyes. "You're very observant."

"You practically ignored them at the table, it was hardly an observation. Not to mention the fact that I never heard the end of Lucien's story."

"I am the heir to the throne. I'm my mother's only son. I've been put in situations they could never understand. I've been asked to take on things they could never take on. They've done nothing but take what royalty has to offer them. I quit being their brother years ago."

She studied me closely, as if she was looking for a lie in my words.

"Adeline seems nice. Is that all fake, too?" she asked.

I smiled. It felt like the first time all day. "No, it's not fake. You can trust Adeline. She just might hate this just as much as I do."

"Hate what?"

"The parties. The royalty. The facade. It's all just a game to these people. They never step foot into the real world. They live here in this bubble and don't care about what happens to the others."

"And you're so different?"

I clicked my tongue. "You're very inquisitive, princess."

"It seems I have a lot to learn, *prince*, and if history tells us anything, I may not have much time to learn it all."

"You're also stubborn."

"I've been told."

When the song was over, Jade stepped away. "You should get back to your party. I'm going to find something to eat," she said.

Shit. I had totally forgotten about the food I was supposed to find for her. "Do you want me to find something for you?"

"No," she answered sharply. "I can handle myself, thank you."

I nodded and watched her walk away, back into the sea of vipers.

CHAPTER 7
Jade

I knew he was watching me. I knew he wasn't going to take his eyes off me for the entire night.

But I had to find a way to meet Adonis at midnight.

I was skeptical at first, but he was right. I didn't have any options. Malachi wasn't exactly forthcoming with information about who I should be on the lookout for. And Malachi seemed to respect Adonis enough.

Not like I trusted Malachi's judgment, but still. It was better than nothing.

I kept my head down as I weaved through the crowd. Most of the fae ignored me completely, only a few were brave enough to raise their heads and meet my eyes. Malachi's reputation had seen to that, I was sure.

Whatever reputation he had with the fae was beyond me. But whatever it was, it hadn't been all rumors. Or else his brothers wouldn't have banded against him like that.

Perhaps the rumors I had heard about my dear husband held some truth.

I continued walking the perimeter of the ballroom, but I found myself drawn into the pure magnificence of the building. I had never seen anything like it. Back home, the houses were built with nothing more than wooden scraps. Even the wealthier families had struggled with building anything out of the ordinary.

But this...this was more than I had ever imagined. Even in the grand room, the space felt inviting. The walls were not just bare stone, but they were covered with vines and greenery that moved with the structure. Each doorway was large enough to fit four people at any given time, and the ceilings were arched with an opaque glass that allowed me to see through the ceiling and into the now dark sky.

Someone bumped my shoulder, nearly knocking me off my feet, but I caught myself against the wall. I turned, half expecting to be confronted by another fae, but the culprit just mumbled an apology and kept moving.

"Having a good time?" a woman's voice approached from my left. I snapped my head in her direction, only to find myself staring directly at the gorgeous blonde fae who had been speaking to Malachi earlier.

Great.

I forced a smile and rolled my shoulders back. "As good as possible, I suppose."

The girl smiled and stepped closer. "The fae love their parties. I suppose of all the rumors that live in the human lands, that one is likely the most truthful. I'm Kara by the way."

I studied her face for any ounce of malice, but found nothing. Every word that came from her mouth felt genuine. But if what I saw between her and Malachi earlier was what I thought it was, Kara was just pretending to be nice to me. If anything existed in both the fae and human lands, it was jealousy.

"It's nice to meet you, Kara. And yes, this party certainly does not disappoint after everything I've heard," I said, matching her politeness.

"This must be quite a change from home," she continued. "I can't imagine leaving fae and continuing life in the human lands."

Was that a diss? Or was she being genuine?

"The human lands weren't much, but they were home."

Kara took a sip of her drink and flipped her long hair over her shoulder. Her dress was even more scandalous than my own, exposing most of her tanned skin. "Rewyth can be tough at times, but it's home. If you find yourself needing a friend here, I'm never too far."

I hid my shock as much as possible. Not only was she a fae interacting with a human, but she clearly had some sort of past with Malachi. Nonetheless, I needed as many allies as possible.

"That's very kind of you, thank you. Although I'm not entirely sure how much freedom I'll be permitted here," I said.

Kara laughed. "Malachi can be possessive, that much is true. But you're a smart girl, Jade. I can tell. You'll figure it out."

Now it was my turn to laugh. "You sound pretty confident for someone who just met me."

Kara leaned in to whisper, "You remind me a lot of myself, Jade. But I must warn you– Malachi isn't the brooding, obedient prince everyone takes him for. He's a crack of lightning in the middle of a thunderstorm. Be very careful."

I didn't have time to question what she meant. She winked at me and disappeared in the crowd, her dress flowing on the ground behind her.

Okay, this night was getting weird.

What in the Saints did that mean? Adeline had told me I could trust Malachi, but Kara was telling me the opposite?

I caught myself frowning and straightened immediately, replacing the slip of emotions with a delighted, ignorant mask.

Kara wasn't going to mess with my head. I knew what I was doing. I took a few steps toward the massive doorways. It was almost midnight. Adonis would be waiting for me, and after the conversation I just had with Kara, I was desperate.

Nobody seemed to be paying attention. Everyone was busy dancing or drinking until they passed out. I dipped my head and slipped through the doorway, into the dark hallway.

A few rings of laughter echoed against the stone walls. I froze, but nobody approached. I kept my ears peeled for any sign of approaching footsteps.

Saints. Would I even be able to hear a fae if one tried to sneak up on me?

I walked slowly, but my shoes still clicked on the floor. I knelt down and slid them both off. My plan wasn't about to get ruined because of some stupid high heels.

The floor was cold against my feet, but it was refreshing. It was like a wave of cool water rushing through me, electrifying my senses.

I didn't so much as breathe as I snaked through the shadows, counting the doorways as I passed them. Adonis would be waiting here, I just had to make it a few more feet until–

A strong hand grabbed my arm and yanked me sideways, sucking me into a shadow-filled doorway. I would have gasped if it weren't for a strong hand covering my mouth and forcing away any scream for help.

I fought to get free in the dark hallway we were pulled into, but the arm that wasn't covering my mouth pinned my arms to my sides and forced me against his body.

"Be quiet, dammit!" Malachi's voice whispered roughly in my ear.

I needed to scream out. I needed to get free. I

needed to do something–anything. Because I wasn't going to die here. I wasn't going to let him ruin my entire plan.

I was seconds away from biting his hand to scream for help when a group of footsteps rushed into the hallway.

"Where is she?" a man asked. No, I knew that voice. It was Adonis.

"She came this way, I swear!" one of the other brothers chirped.

"I told her to meet us here at midnight," Adonis's voice echoed through the hallway. I stiffened. Mal's hand didn't leave my mouth.

They were talking about me.

"Maybe she's not quite as stupid as the others," another one of the brothers asked.

This earned a laugh from the rest of them.

Were all of the brothers out there looking for me?

"Do you think she told Malachi what you said?" The brother asked.

"I doubt it. She doesn't trust a soul right now, and after I was done talking to her, she practically reeked of fear. She won't tell Malachi anything."

Now it was Malachi's turn to tense behind me.

Okay. If I wasn't dead earlier, I was definitely dead now.

The footsteps approached us, and I was prepared for them to walk into the same dark room as us. But they passed us by, echoing into the distance until they eventually grew silent.

My husband released the death grip he held on me and I let out a long breath.

"What was that?" I breathed, whirling to face him. "Why are you hiding from them?"

He grabbed my shoulders and shoved my back against the wall, pinning me there. "What did he tell you?" He asked, his dark eyes piercing into me. I hesitated. Malachi saw it, too. "I can smell lies, princess, so think wisely about what you're about to say."

I debated my options. Telling Malachi what Adonis said would ensure that I couldn't sneak away to meet with him. But Malachi clearly had reasons not to trust his brothers. Did that mean that I shouldn't, either?

After what I had just heard, I wasn't so sure meeting with Adonis was going to help me at all.

Malachi's body was inches from mine, and he pressed a hand on the wall on either side of my head. The room was too dark to see anything, but I could feel his breath on my cheek.

I knew he could see me, though. I knew he was tracking every emotion that flickered across my face. And he was furious.

The truth might be my only way out of this situation alive.

"Fine," I admitted. "Adonis told me I couldn't trust you. He said he would meet me out here at midnight, and that he could help me."

"Help you?"

"That's what he said." Malachi backed away and

ran a hand through his hair. "Were those the rest of your brothers with him?" I asked.

He took a long breath before mumbling, "Yeah. Yeah, it was."

"What do you think they were doing? Why would all of them try to meet with me alone in an empty room?"

"I don't know, dammit!" Malachi said, temper clearly unraveling. He clenched his fists as he paced back and forth in the dark room. "If you would have just stayed by my side like I ordered you to do, we wouldn't be in this situation. You knowingly put yourself in danger, Jade!"

"Excuse me? Like you *ordered* me?"

"You are my wife, Jade Farrow. If I tell you to do something, it's an *order.*"

I couldn't believe what I was hearing. I pushed myself off the wall, heart pounding in my chest. "If you think I'm just another one of your stupid human wives who will let you boss them around, you're wrong. And I'm sorry your family is messed up and your brothers are clearly not very supportive, but grow up. It's not my fault someone wants me dead. You seem to care enough about me to not kill me yourself, which somehow doesn't make me feel any better. We've all got issues, Malachi. Don't think for a second you can boss me around and treat me like trash just because I'm not fae."

My voice had grown to a yell, but I didn't back away.

Malachi took a step closer. "Then let me get one

thing straight, *wife*. You think I care about you? That's cute. I don't care about you. I don't care about your past, and I certainly don't care about your future." He spoke in a way that shook my bones. It was pure power. Pure anger. "But someone wants you dead. That creates a few problems for me, and the main problem is that someone close to me has been betraying me. I'm going to find out who that is, which will be impossible if you walk away from me and get yourself killed before I find out who it is! So, when I order you to stay by my side, you stay by my side next time. Got it?"

I clenched my jaw. How stupid was I to think Malachi was actually an honorable man who wanted to keep his wife safe? Who wanted to uphold his vows. *Dammit, Jade.* Of course he didn't care about me. I was *human*.

I was nothing but a temporary toy to the fae.

In this case, I was nothing but a tool for Malachi's master plan.

I had to remember what my goal was. Tessa would starve if I died. I was here for a reason, and I had to survive. If that meant going along with whatever plan Malachi had, then so be it.

Even if it absolutely killed me to admit it.

"Fine," I said after a few seconds. "I'm sorry I left you. It won't happen again."

He considered my words for a moment, and I could feel him examining my face in the darkness. I shivered.

"No," he growled. "It *won't* happen again."

Before I could protest, he grabbed my wrist and walked out of the room, dragging me behind him.

Except he didn't take us back to the ballroom.

"Where are we going?" I asked.

His steps were fast and aggressive. I had to jog so I wouldn't fall straight on my face.

As we snaked through the cascading hallways of the castle, it dawned on me where Malachi was going to take me.

It was his wedding night. *Our* wedding night. He was taking me to his bedroom.

The pit that formed in my stomach was confirmation enough. I had expected this. From the moment my father told me I was being sent to marry the fae prince, I expected this moment. Prepared for it mentally.

But Malachi was pissed. That wasn't exactly helping my nerves.

He didn't say anything else. Just continued dragging me through the castle in silence.

When we rounded the last corner, we weren't alone in the hallway. I rolled my shoulders back and lifted my chin as Malachi approached the guard that stood in front of what I assumed to be his bedroom door.

I had seen that guard before, I thought to myself. His dark skin contrasted with the white stone walls. He was tall, but still had a comforting posture. He turned to us as we approached, and his face came into view. He was the guard that took me from my home.

Serefin.

"My lord," Serefin greeted Malachi as we

approached. He gave me a small nod of acknowledgment before returning his attention to Malachi. "I believe congratulations are now in order," he chirped.

I half expected Malachi to yell, but he just clasped Serefin on the shoulder and laughed, finally letting go of my wrist.

"If you even think about it, I'll kill you," Malachi joked. The two of them laughed, and I found myself surprised that the Prince of Shadows interacted with anyone this way. It was intimate and personal, they had clearly been friends for quite some time. "You're lucky you get to miss stupid parties like that."

I rolled my eyes behind him. Of course he would describe the biggest and worst day of my life as a *stupid party*.

But I was merely a human. My life was expendable to him.

"Something wrong?" Serefin asked, calling me out. I supposed my annoyance wasn't as subtle as I expected it to be.

"Nothing's wrong," I replied, but the words somehow added to the fuel of my anger. Malachi turned to face me, eyebrow arched. "Being dragged out of my house before dawn this morning only to have my entire life ruined by a *stupid party* full of people who may or may not want to kill me is exactly how I imagined this day. Thanks for asking, Serefin."

He didn't respond. Just gave Malachi a glance that said *good luck with that*.

"My wife has had quite a day," Malachi said. "But I

have a feeling the night is far from over. Are you on guard all night?"

Serefin checked that the hallways were empty before answering, "So far, yes. I had to bribe Darcy to switch posts with me, though. He was pretty hesitant, I guess your father has everyone on pretty strict orders tonight."

Malachi sighed and tilted his head back, eyes closed. "I wish I could say that was surprising," he said.

"You think the King has something to do with this?" Serefin whispered.

Mal clenched his jaw then moved to open the bedroom door. "Let's talk in here," he said. Serefin nodded, and the three of us entered Malachi's bedroom.

I did my best to appear relaxed and confident, but as soon as I walked through the door, I was amazed. What was I expecting? Skulls and black everything? *Yes.*

Malachi's room was spectacular. The ceiling was nearly transparent, similar to the ceiling in the ball-room. Greenery and vines twisted their way around the dark stone of the walls, and a large, four-post bed with black, silk sheets anchored in the center of the room. A bathroom in the back of the room consisted of a water-fall-like structure, the greenery and stones mimicking nature almost to perfection.

Serefin and Malachi were oblivious to my reaction, which saved me a decent amount of embarrassment. They walked into the room as I lingered by the door.

"My father was insistent on me trusting everyone at

the party. He practically told me not to worry about Jade's safety," Malachi said.

"So, you think he wants Jade's safety to be compromised? Maybe he's just a prick and didn't want his ego to take a hit by you not trusting his guards."

"Maybe, but I also found my *brothers* looking for Jade in the hallway earlier. Adonis wanted to meet with her *alone*."

"What?" Serefin asked, spinning to look at me. "Why? What did he want?"

I lifted my hands in defeat. If I knew, I wouldn't have gone to meet him like an idiot.

"You can't trust them," Serefin warned me. He looked between Malachi and me. "You told her she can't trust them, right?"

"That seems to be a common warning around here," I mumbled.

"You don't think they have anything to do with the murders, do you?"

"I don't know. I can't be sure about anything anymore."

Serefin nodded. "I'll be on guard all night. I'll let you know if I run into any problems."

"Thanks, Ser," Mal replied. "This is going to be a long night. Nobody's laying a hand on her."

"Agreed," Serefin said. An unsaid agreement crossed between them. I could tell Serefin meant it. He was loyal to Malachi. I might not have trusted a single soul in the castle, but Serefin trusted Malachi, and

Serefin might have been the only person that Malachi actually trusted.

Either way, I knew Serefin would do his best to keep his word. Even if I wasn't sure I could trust Malachi yet.

Serefin moved to open the door but paused and looked at me. "By the way, you make a beautiful bride Jade," he said.

Heat rushed to my face, but he was already out of the room, closing the door behind him.

Leaving Malachi and I alone in his bedroom.

CHAPTER 8

Malachi

"You're welcome to stand there all night, but it might get a bit uncomfortable," I said. Jade had been standing there for the past five minutes as if that was going to somehow protect her.

She rolled her eyes and stepped away from her spot near the door.

"Is anyone going to miss us at the party?" she asked.

I huffed and shrugged off my thick jacket. "That party wasn't for us. It was just an excuse to get drunk and party all night. They won't be stopping anytime soon."

"That's reassuring," she mumbled. Her words were strong but she crossed her arms over chest and refused to look at me. She looked at the bed, the couch, the walls. Anywhere but me.

It hadn't dawned on me that Jade would be nervous about sleeping in here. After all the rumors she had heard about me before, certainly she expected something to come from tonight.

I wanted to reassure her, but stopped myself before I opened my mouth. Jade should be afraid. It was good that she had her guard up. None of my other wives had made it this far into the night. That might have been because we all over-indulged in the fae wine each time.

"We'll both have to stay here the whole night," I said, forcing myself to say *something*. "If you sleep in another room, I won't be able to protect you. This is the best option."

"I understand," she said, walking over and sitting on the edge of my bed.

"Besides," I continued. "I already get enough shit from my father. I don't need to give them any more reasons to doubt me."

She opened her mouth like she was about to say something, but closed it again.

My chest tightened. She really *was* terrified. It was surprising, I had to admit. This was the same girl that launched herself at a wolf over a tiny dead rabbit, and she was afraid to be in a room with me.

She wasn't the least bit afraid of me in the woods. Granted, she didn't know I was fae.

A tiny shiver rumbled down her spine, one that she tried to hide.

"You're cold?" I asked.

She shook her head. *Liar.*

I walked to my closet and pulled out a shirt and

pants. They would be huge on her, but it was better than wearing the gold wedding dress all night.

The dress I was sure Adeline had something to do with.

"Here," I said, tossing them into her lap. She looked relieved when she realized what it was. "Bathroom's that way. Use whatever you need."

She stood and walked toward the bathroom with her head down, but paused and turned around. "You're not going to kill me while I'm in the shower, are you?"

I laughed. "If I wanted to kill you, princess, you'd be dead right now."

She gave a sarcastic smile before mumbling under her breath and walking into the bathroom.

I took a long breath. We had made it this far, which was a good sign. But something was definitely going on with my brothers.

And Jade had actually trusted Adonis over me. I knew she wasn't going to trust me right away, but trusting one of them was going to be more dangerous for her than anything.

My brothers never had my best interests in mind. *Never.*

I listened to the bathroom until I heard Jade step under the stream of water. My mind wandered to the thought of her standing there, water trickling over her perfect black hair. She was beautiful, that much was true. She was different from the other humans who had been sent to marry me, somehow owing a debt to my father and thinking this would make up for it.

Jade was defiant. She wasn't planning on listening to anything I said. I still wasn't entirely convinced that she was actually afraid of the fae, but maybe she was at least pretending to be afraid for her own safety. She had survival instincts. When I saw her for the first time in the forest with the wolves, I knew she would be hard for anyone to try and kill. Jade had a certain fire to her that annoyed me to no end.

If she would just trust me, keeping her alive would be a lot easier.

But what was I supposed to say? I couldn't tell her that the rumors weren't true. I couldn't tell her that I wasn't the horrific, violent Prince of Shadows she had heard about. I couldn't tell her those things because they weren't true.

The things I did to survive were less than admirable. But Jade had those same instincts. Maybe she would understand.

Or maybe she would hate me for everything I had done. She probably already did. I couldn't ask her what she had heard about me. Saints, did I even care? People had been spreading rumors about me longer than Jade had been alive. For years, I had heard about the Prince of Shadows who could kill an entire room of fae with just a look. I had heard about the Saint-cursed fae with black wings who was touched by the demons. I had heard about the slave of the king who carried out his assassinations with ease and delight.

The stories had gotten so ridiculous, Serefin and I had often sat down and joked about how twisted they became. But that's the thing about rumors. Truth is usually mixed in there somewhere.

"How's it going in there?" I asked.

"I am very capable of taking showers without the need for you to check up on me, thanks," she yelled from the bathroom.

Great.

I tugged my shirt off and threw it into my closet, lying back on the bed. The stars were bright tonight. That was one thing I actually admired about Rewyth: the stars. They were brighter here than anything else I had ever seen. It was why half the castle was built with transparent ceilings. The view was too beautiful to ignore.

It was a view I would fight for.

Amongst other things.

My thoughts were interrupted when Jade stepped out of the bathroom. Wearing my clothes. With dripping wet hair.

Saints save me.

"Nice shower," she chirped.

I nodded, trying not to stare. "Our ancestors wanted us to be connected to nature. I like it. Reminds me of where we come from."

"And where's that?" she asked.

"You have a lot to learn about the history of fae. We didn't always reside here. The fae had to fight for this land. There was a time when fae weren't at all powerful. We were the weakest of the creatures. We fought for decades to claim our power. To claim our lands."

She listened as I talked.

"Many fae used to believe we drew our power from the elements. It's not practiced as much anymore, but it used to be. Fae would partner with witches and warlocks to strengthen their gifts."

"Gifts?" she asked.

I nodded. "Some fae have special gifts. Magic, I guess. But not everyone."

Jade walked around the bed and sat on the edge, as far from me as possible. Her eyes flickered to my bare chest.

"I won't bite, you know. You may think whatever you'd like about me, but I'm not going to touch you."

She nodded but didn't move. Clearly she didn't trust me. It made me wonder if another man had ever hurt her before. And that made me want to storm right back to the human lands and rip the head off anyone who did.

Jade interrupted my thoughts with, "Can I ask you a question, Malachi?"

"Depends on the question."

"You don't look like fae. None of you do. On the way here, Serefin told me you used..."

"Glamour?" I finished for her. "We all do. It's simple magic to make us appear normal."

"But why? You're in your own castle, why wouldn't you just be yourself?"

The question made me smile. "It's a simple trick so you would feel more relaxed. It's bad enough that we drag a young woman into our castle and force her to marry. Better not scare you with our looks."

She scoffed. "How noble of you."

A feral sense of competition creeped into me. Jade was challenging me. She was challenging my words. Stupid, stubborn human. I rolled off the bed and walked around to her side, inches from where she sat. "Would you like to see what the fae really look like, princess?"

She swallowed once.

"Or are you afraid?"

"I'm not afraid," she answered quickly.

I stepped closer, looking down to where she sat on the bed. "No?" I teased.

Jade lifted her chin and stared at me with those big, endless eyes. "Let me see," she said.

I couldn't tell if it was fake confidence or simple arrogance.

But I didn't care. If Jade was going to survive the night, she was going to have to learn what she was up against.

With a single breath, I dropped the glamour that was concealing my fae characteristics. The glamour that hid my large, uniquely black wings. The glamour that hid the points in my ears.

Jade's eyes widened. I growled and spread my wings, nearly covering us both with the sheer size.

"Well?" I asked. "What do you think?"

Her eyes dragged across my torso and drank up

every new detail. She wasn't afraid like I had expected her to be.

No, she was feeling something else. She stood from where she sat on the edge of the bed, her head just meeting the top of my chest despite the fact that she was tall for a human.

Slowly, Jade smiled. Wicked curiosity washed over her face. "They call you the Prince of Shadows for a reason, I see."

"They call me that because of more than just the color of my wings, princess."

Her eyes snapped to mine. "Don't call me princess."

"Why not? Like it or not, that's what you are now. Princess of Rewyth."

"Let's just worry about surviving the night first."

"You doubt my abilities to protect you?"

"I doubt my safety in the presence of fae."

The silence that rang though the air said more than I could form with words.

Jade still didn't trust me. I guessed that was fair.

But we had a few hours to go until sunrise, and it was her and I in this room alone until then.

I moved my wings in a motion that blew her hair across her face.

She gasped and scrambled to get it out of her eyes while I laughed.

"You think this is funny?" She snapped "You really have fun toying with worthless humans, don't you?"

"Calm down, princess. We're both in a shitty situation here. You might as well lighten up."

"You can't be serious."

"Serious as ever."

"Please explain to me, prince, how this could possibly be a shitty situation for you? You basically get hand delivered a wife, a party thrown in your favor, and eligibility for your own Kingdom. What part of that is shitty for you?"

I stepped back, finally putting some distance in between us. "It's complicated," was all I had the energy to say.

"Right; because your dumb human of a wife can't understand anything complicated."

"You really should get some sleep," I said, walking to the other side of the room. "I'll wake you if I hear anything."

To my surprise, Jade actually got back into bed. It had to be from pure exhaustion, because Jade was too stubborn to do anything I suggested.

I listened to her breathing as it slowed.

It was only after I was sure she was asleep that I turned around to look at her.

I smiled when I saw her curled up in my bed, clutching the knife I had gifted her as if it were her only hope in this world.

CHAPTER 9
Jade

I woke up with a panic. Sweat dampened my forehead. Falling asleep was certainly not part of the plan, especially when my life was at risk. But I was still holding my weapon, *my wedding gift*, which was a good sign.

Perhaps Malachi let me keep it in case we *were* really attacked here tonight. Or maybe it was because my little knife was nothing against a fae. Maybe he knew I wasn't even a threat against him with it.

I sat up and caught him already staring at me from the chair across the room. "You snore," he spat.

Ignoring him, I flung the blankets off my legs and stood up. Although I didn't remember getting under the blankets in the first place.

"It's been quiet so far," Malachi continued. "No sign of anything unusual. Serefin is still outside the door. Nothing from him, either."

I nodded and folded my arms across my chest.

Malachi was still shirtless, and his black wings hung casually off each side of the large sofa.

Part of me was grateful that he had waited to show me until we were alone. I was certain I had looked like an idiot, mouth gaping and everything.

But if I was being honest, Malachi looked terrifying with those things. I had heard the stories about the Prince of Shadows and his dark wings, which obviously stood out in a fae land with silver wings. But I wasn't going to ask about them.

Malachi's ego was big enough already.

I looked away before he caught me staring.

I walked to the large glass window, staring up at the stars that littered the sky.

"Careful," Malachi warned. "You don't want an arrow in the chest because you're admiring the stars."

I blushed, as if somehow Mal realizing what I was doing made me appear weak.

"You really think someone will try to kill me while I'm with you?"

"Yes," he said without hesitating. His dark eyes seemed to grow even darker, swarming with emotion and exhaustion. "I do."

I ran my hands through my hair and let out a long breath. "How were they killed?" I asked, crossing the room to sit next to him on the long sofa. "Your wives, I mean."

"I know what you meant," he said quietly. His eyes remained somewhere in the distance. "We found my first wife with a slit throat in the hallway during the party," he said. "Nobody saw, nobody knew anything. We had all continued to drink like idiots, who knows how long she had been dead."

I remained silent.

"My second wife was strangled while I slept next to her. Someone had drugged my drinks, I didn't find her until I woke up nearly a day later."

More silence.

"My third wife didn't even make it to the ceremony. I guess that doesn't technically make her a wife, but it all meant the same."

I hid my shock.

"Who would want your wives dead?" I asked, careful with my choice of tone.

"That list is very long, princess. I've earned quite a few enemies in my days."

I thought for a moment. Each of his wives had died long before now. Why was someone waiting so long to make an attempt on me?

As if on cue, Malachi's pointed ears flickered up. I opened my mouth to ask what he was hearing, but the look he gave me made me close my mouth.

I double checked the knife I had strapped back to my thigh. Someone was here.

"Act like we're still having a normal conversation," he whispered.

I nodded and smiled. "Okay," I said. I didn't risk looking out the window.

Malachi reached his arm up and over, placing it

around my shoulder. He moved his body so I was tucked into his side.

"Is everything okay?" I asked when he was close enough.

He picked up a strand of my hair and leaned in. To anyone watching from the window, it would look like he was kissing my neck.

Still, every single one of my senses was aware of his every move.

"When I say go, I want you to roll under the bed," he whispered, lips brushing my ear. "And don't come out until I come get you."

I let him lean over me, pushing my torso back and reclining both of us until his entire body was covering my own on the couch.

I couldn't speak. I just nodded.

He slid a hand up my thigh, finding the knife that he had gifted me. My skin lit up under his touch.

"I hope you know how to use that thing, princess," he mumbled. He was so close, I was certain he was going to kiss me again.

His eyes moved to my lips, only for a split second, before the sound of shattering glass erupted in the air.

"NOW!" Malachi yelled, launching into action. Before I could even sit up, Mal was across the room. Two fae, dressed head to toe in black, concealing armor busted through the opened window.

Malachi dropped on them in seconds. He held a small dagger in each hand. Where had he been keeping those? He dodged each advance with little effort. He towered over both of his attackers by at least a foot, but they kept his attention on them

I was still cowered on the couch like an idiot.

Under the bed, Jade. Get under the bed.

Saints, where was Serefin?

I rolled sideways and crawled on all fours toward the bed. I had almost made it, too, when rough hands grabbed me by the ankles and dragged me backward.

I screamed and kicked as hard as I could, but my attacker just launched himself on top of me, pinning me to the ground.

I searched for Malachi in the dark room, but saw him fighting hand to hand with the other attacker.

A rough hand grabbed my hair, pulling my head backward.

"Please don't," I begged. "I have a family to take care of!"

The man laughed. It was rough and ugly. "Unfortunately for you, so do I."

I felt the cold steel of a blade against my neck.

This was it. I hadn't fought hard enough. I didn't try hard enough.

I was going to die.

Warm liquid poured over my back, and my attacker went still.

"Are you okay?" Malachi asked.

My heart pounded. I waited for the weight to lift off my back before I turned over.

Both attackers were dead.

And Malachi held a severed head.

I couldn't talk. I could barely breathe. I backed up slowly, scooting away from the pool of blood that I was now covered with. It dripped down my back, still hot.

Serefin busted through the bedroom door. He took one glance at Malachi, holding the severed head, and cursed. It was then that I noticed Serefin also splattered with blood, and his sword already drawn.

"We're okay," Malachi informed him. "Two of them came through the window. They didn't even wait until I was asleep."

"Bastards," Serefin mumbled. He walked to the body that was still intact and rolled it over. Malachi had stabbed him in the chest. "There was one in the hallway. He ran off after I landed a blow, but I heard Jade's scream."

"Do you recognize them?" Malachi asked. Serefin shook his head.

"Someone in this castle will, though."

Serefin stood up and looked at me. I cowered into the corner, my entire body still shaking from what just happened.

"You okay, princess?" Malachi asked again, finally dropping the head he had been holding. It rolled to the side with a sickening thump.

I nodded yes, but I was sure they knew I was lying. I should be dead right now. What Malachi just did, the speed at which he moved....it wasn't possible.

Malachi had ripped that man's head off within a second.

It was pure feral behavior. Pure predator.

Serefin and Malachi exchanged a knowing glance.

Mal walked over and knelt beside me, lifting my chin with a finger.

"People want you dead, Jade. They want you dead so badly that they'd risk fighting against me to get to you."

His eyes were intense, and I sat in silence as his focus moved from my face down to my throat.

He reached out and rubbed a thumb against my skin. It stung, but I didn't flinch. I hardly felt it.

When he pulled away, his thumb dripped with my blood.

His wings flared once more, and he drew his eyebrows together in an intense expression that nearly made me look away.

"You're hurt," he said. It wasn't a question.

"I'm fine." My words sounded foreign.

"Don't tell me you're fine. You're bleeding."

He balled his hand to a fist and stood up slowly, looking between me and Serefin.

"Those bastards drew blood," he announced. "The people in this room are the only people we tell about this. Nobody else finds out until we know who we can trust."

Serefin nodded.

"If anyone so much as lifts a finger toward Jade, I will kill them. And I'll have *fun* ripping their heads from their useless bodies."

CHAPTER 10
Malachi

"What about your father?" Serefin asked.

"Someone expects Jade to be dead. Get rid of the bodies. Let's go see who's surprised when they see her alive and well," I said.

The next few hours mixed together in a blur of rage and fear.

Serefin took care of the bodies, but Jade didn't take her eyes off the severed head until the bodies were out of view.

I couldn't even look at her. She was covered in blood, most of it not hers. Her black hair had matted with it, and the shirt of mine she wore had ripped at the torso during her struggle.

He never should have touched her. I should have stopped it.

But here we were.

Serefin had left a few minutes ago, but Jade still hadn't moved from the floor.

"You have to eat something," I said in an attempt to break the silence in the room.

She pulled her knees to her chest and wrapped her arms around them.

"Jade," I said again. "You faced an entire pack of wolves over a dead rabbit in the woods. Certainly a couple of rogue men aren't that bad."

I tested the waters, trying to get any reaction out of her. Anything to let me know she was actually alive in there.

"What was that?" she asked. "You didn't even touch them and they..."

"It's a special gift of mine. I can inflict severe pain on anyone with a single thought. It takes focus, but it comes in handy."

She nodded.

Her dark eyes snapped to mine. "That can't happen again," she said, her voice was barely a whisper and I tried not to react when it cracked.

"No," I replied quietly. "It can't, and it won't." She wouldn't even look at me. I wasn't sure if she had been talking about the attack, or me.

"So what do we do? We don't know who wants me dead. We don't even know who those people were who..."

"From now on you'll either be with me or Serefin at all times. It would take an entire army to kill one of us, princess. You're safe. It might not feel like it, but you're safe."

She pushed herself from the ground and stood up. "I want to see my sister," she said.

I waited for a second for her to add something to that statement.

But she just stared at me.

"Absolutely not," I answered.

She scowled and crossed her arms. "She expected me to die last night. I expected to die. I have to tell her I'm okay."

"You're covered in blood and you're cut. You're not going anywhere, especially when we don't know who wants you dead. You're not okay."

I watched her chest rise and fall. If she wasn't in shock yet, she would be soon.

But based on the amount of blood she had yet to wash off, she wasn't handling this well.

"If you take me to see my sister, I'll help you find out who did this. We both want the same thing. Me alive. Do this one thing for me and I'll help you."

Any other day, I would have said no. I would have said Saints no. But even covered in her attackers' blood, Jade was the most stubborn human I had ever met.

That was going to be dangerous. But it could also be useful in the fae court.

I looked at her from head to toe. Her bare feet looked so small against the stone tile of the floor. Her exposed legs were tan, something I was sure she had earned from hunting outside all the time. She was skinny. Too skinny. I was going to have to strengthen her up if she was going to fight off a fae.

And she still held that knife. Her knuckles were white from her grip.

"Fine," I said. I didn't know if it was a lie, or if I was actually giving in. "I'll take you back to your house. But you do everything I tell you, no arguing anymore. And you have to actually trust me if you want to survive in Rewyth, princess. And I decide when we leave, so don't go bugging me about it every day. You're staying here for now."

Her eyes lit up, but she kept her face still. "Don't call me princess," she repeated as she walked past me and into the bathroom. "And quit looking at me like I'm fresh meat. It's not a good look on you."

I waited until I heard her step underneath the water again before I let out the breath I was holding.

Her sass would have annoyed me to no end any other day, but today, I found myself smiling.

She had seen me rip a man's head from his body, and she was still able to crack jokes. That was a good start.

But we had a long way to go if Jade was going to stay alive.

CHAPTER 11
Jade

M alachi had been gone for hours. I spent a majority of the night trying to sleep, but it was impossible.

Everything I thought I knew was wrong, and Malachi had power that I had only heard about in ancient legends.

My mind was spinning. I remembered every single rumor I had ever heard about the Prince of Shadows, and I tried to decipher the truth.

The truth about my husband. The truth about my new life.

My stomach grumbled. What was he out there doing? Where did he go? To find whoever did this, I hoped. But Malachi seemed to have his own agenda. He seemed to have his own ideas about who was behind this attack.

And he wasn't sharing anything with me.

The door had been locked. I checked as soon as

Malachi left. I wasn't surprised. After what happened, he wasn't going to let me out of here. I was as good as dead.

"I know you're out there," I yelled through the door. My forehead felt hot as I laid in against the surface of the door. "You can't just leave me in here and expect me to sit quietly. I'm hungry!"

I heard movement before Serefin responded, "Just wait a few more hours. I'm sure the prince will be back soon."

My stomach sank. "Hours? You really want me to sit in here alone every day just waiting for Malachi to come home?" I took a deep breath and tried to calm my emotions, but my throat was stinging. "I didn't survive this far to sit here and rot in a bedroom that isn't even mine."

Tears threatened my eyes. I placed both palms against the door and imagined bursting through it, bursting all the way out of this damn castle. My words were true. I didn't survive longer than any human wife before me to just sit here and rot like some sort of prisoner.

I was Malachi's wife. I was a princess to Rewyth. I hated that title, but I sure as saints was going to use it to my advantage if I had to.

Before I could open my mouth to plead with Serefin once more, the doorhandle began rattling.

I backed away as Serefin entered, shutting the door behind him.

"I can't let you leave," he said. His eyes assessed the situation, and I saw the tiniest bit of pity in them.

"You feel sorry for me?" I asked.

"I would feel sorry for anyone who's going through what you're going through. Nobody should have to live here against their will."

I laughed. "Even a retched, useless human? Aren't all fae supposed to hate us, anyway? What makes you so different?"

Serefin walked over to my open window and pushed it shut. He turned to face me before answering, "Not all fae think that way, Jade. That would be like you thinking all fae are evil, malicious beings. And you don't think that, do you?"

I held his gaze. Serefin was nearly as tall as Malachi, with now-visible silver wings that tucked tightly behind his shoulder blades. His black guard uniform was perfectly aligned to his slim body. Serefin wasn't my enemy. If anything, Serefin had been kind to me when he had no reason to be. He had shown me mercy.

I took a seat on the large sofa, but Serefin didn't move from the window. "I don't think you're evil, no," I answered with caution.

Serefin smiled. "Good. Then we're off to a good start, princess."

I tossed my head back and groaned.

"What?" he asked. "You don't want to be a princess?"

"That's a joke, right?" I replied. "In what world

would I want to be a princess in a place where everyone wants me dead."

Serefin paused as if he were debating whether or not to stay. But after a few seconds, he sighed and came to sit with me on the sofa.

"Malachi's not so bad, you know," he said.

This forced another groan from me. "Yeah, and everyone seems to keep reminding me of that. But he's still the Prince of Shadows, Serefin." I paused and shook my head, remembering the way he killed those men with no more than a blink of an eye. "He's dangerous."

"But he's a great ally," Serefin argued.

My head was spinning. "What type of ally would lock me in a bedroom for an unknown amount of time?"

"You know he just wants to protect you."

"This isn't protecting me," I replied. "I'm a sitting duck here. If anything, this is more dangerous than the alternative."

"The alternative?" Serefin questioned. "You mean it's more dangerous than following Malachi around the kingdom to handle his court business? You really want to do that?"

I thought about it for a moment. "What type of court business does Malachi do, anyway?"

Serefin stood up and walked toward the door. "If you want to know so badly," he said, "then you should probably ask your husband." He grinned, and I caught myself wondering how old Serefin really was. He didn't look much older than me, but fae lived for centuries, nearly immortal.

Serefin could have been hundreds of years older than me. And Malachi, for that matter.

"It's a little hard to ask him anything when he leaves me locked in here."

Serefin turned toward the door and opened it. "You better hurry up then," he asked. "We're going to get dinner."

CHAPTER 12
Malachi

My heart was pounding. It hadn't stopped pounding since the almost deadly attack on Jade.

It had gotten too close. The fact that blood had been drawn was already too much.

I had slept in an empty bedroom across the hall the past couple of nights, but it didn't stop my mind from wandering to Jade's wet hair from the shower, the way she looked at me when I showed her my wings.

Saints help me.

I walked down the empty hallway to my father's quarters. I had spent hours debating on whether or not to trust him with the incident, and my mind was still shouting warnings at me.

My father wasn't going to help me.

He didn't help me with any of my other wives. Not even Laura. So, there was no way he was going to help me now.

Laugh in my face? Maybe. Help me? Not a chance.

But this castle was a snake pit. At the end of the day, my father was the King. If I wanted to stay alive, I had to play by their rules.

"Malachi!" A female voice echoed through the empty hallway. "Wait up!"

I turned around and found Kara running toward me.

A sigh escaped me. "Not now, Kara," I said, turning around and continuing toward my father's quarters.

"Your wife seems like a nice girl," she continued. "I'd love to get to know her more one day."

I stopped dead in my tracks. "You talked to Jade?"

She caught up with me, her blonde hair bouncing as she jogged the last few feet.

"At your wedding, yeah," she said. Another breath escaped me, but my heart was still pounding. "She's pretty, too. Although for a human she's awfully..."

"If I were you, I would be very careful about what you say next, Kara."

She looked at me in awe, then scoffed. "I can't believe this," she said. "You're really going to drop everything we have for another human. I thought you were done with that. After what happened with Laura, I figured you had learned your lesson."

Kara was stupid, but not that stupid. She was trying to get me angry.

I turned and continued walking, but she grabbed my arm. It took every ounce of my strength to resist throwing her small body to the ground.

"What lesson is that, exactly?" I growled.

Kara smiled, but it was calculated. "That what you need is right here, Malachi. You don't have to keep doing this."

"Doing what, Kara?" I ripped my arm from her grip. "I'm not the one deciding I should get married to a human again and again. I'm not the one making those decisions."

Anger flashed across her face. If I had learned one thing about Kara, it was that she couldn't hide her emotions. That type of flaw was deadly in Rewyth.

"You're more powerful than them. You know you are. If you decided what to do with your own life, they would have no choice but to listen."

I shook my head. Kara, just like everyone else, had no idea what they were talking about. They didn't know the power my father had over me.

Of course I was stronger than him. I was stronger than everyone. I could kill any one of them with my power, but then what?

My mother needed me.

My father was my only link to her.

"Leave me alone," I mumbled to her. "You have no clue what you're talking about."

She didn't follow me as I stormed away, but that didn't stop her from yelling, "She'll never belong here, Malachi!"

My vision darkened and my fists clenched.

Jade belonged wherever I said she belonged.

I pushed my father's door open before my anger forced me to turn back around.

He sat alone, drinking from a golden mug in his massive study. "Malachi!" he cheered. "What a nice surprise!"

I shut the door behind me and continued inside the room. His guards didn't move an inch.

They were smarter than him.

"I haven't seen you in a few days," I started. "Anything new I should be aware of?"

He stood from the long wooden table

"Nothing comes to mind."

"Really? Anything regarding my mother, perhaps?" I leaned against the wooden frame of the door.

My father shook his head. "You know the deal, Malachi."

"The deal was that I do what you ask. Well, I married the human–again. So I think it's about time you hold up your side of this bargain. Where is my mother?"

"Patience, boy," he said, standing from his chair. "Marrying the girl is not the end of the road. You should know that more than anyone."

Anger rumbled in my chest. I urged my power back to its core, reigning it in.

"How long are we going to play this game?" I asked.

My father just laughed. "It's no game, son. I'm running a kingdom here. You'll understand one day. You'll understand all the sacrifices I've made for you. And you'll come back to thank me."

It was my turn to laugh. "Thank you?" I repeated. "For what, exactly?"

"For protecting you. There are hundreds if not thousands of people who will enslave you and use your power for their own will. Are you not aware of the war happening across the sea?"

"They'd have to catch me first." I crossed my arms over my chest.

He took a step closer to me and shook his head. "You're just like her. Defiant. Arrogant."

My mother. I couldn't even remember what she looked like. It had been that long since he hid her away, claiming to protect her.

I had spent decades obeying his every order in hopes that he would eventually tell me where she was.

And we had gotten nowhere.

"I'll tell you everything you want to know," he started, "soon. But I need you to trust me."

He placed his hand on my shoulder and squeezed. It wasn't often that I saw this side of him. The side of him that created a king hundreds of years ago.

He hadn't always been terrible. It was hard to believe, but it was true.

"Fine," I said after a while. "But leave Jade alone. She has no part in this."

He nodded in agreement, and I was out the door.

It took a few seconds for my breathing to slow down.

My father knew exactly what he was doing. Saints, I

might have done the same thing. But to my own son? That was a stretch.

One step after another, my feet pounded the stone floor of the compound. How many times had I walked these stupid halls, reporting to my father what mission had been successful? How many of his enemies had I killed? How many wars had I won for him?

And how much information had he given me about what happened to my mother?

I shook my head. This wasn't the time for anger. I had to play this one smart. If he had anything to do with Jade's attack, he would attack again.

And soon.

I heard her before I saw her.

Jade's voice echoed through the stone walls of the dining hall. My feet moved toward her like I had no choice.

What in the Saints was she doing down here?

I turned the corner just in time to see her tossing her head back in laughter, that red line on her throat still visible. She was sitting next to Serefin, which instantly made me relax.

But it wasn't Serefin and Jade that concerned me. It was everyone else.

"This has to be some sort of record," my brother Eli asked her. Nobody looked at me as I approached, lurking as far back as possible.

Jade smiled, but her eyes remained focused. "Are you surprised, dear brother?"

The way she spoke to him made my stomach flip. It

was bold for any human to talk to a fae that way. Even if that human was my wife.

Eli sat back in his chair, and the rest of my brothers laughed. The dining room was filled with spectators. Nobody would dare make a move here, but still. Serefin was tense, his eyes tracked every single one of my brother's movements.

I trusted him with my life. I had no doubt that he would keep Jade safe.

But why the Saints would he bring her here? Sitting around, waiting for an attack?

Kara entered the room, trotting over to the table as if she owned the place. She pulled up the seat on the other side of Serefin and beckoned one of the servants for a plate of food.

I took a step back, ensuring I was hidden in the shadows of the hallway.

"What have I missed?" she sneered. How had I not noticed how annoying her voice was?

My brothers were still laughing amongst themselves, but Adonis leaned forward. "We're just making the acquaintance of our dear sister," he said. "Someone attempted to take her life the other day. Did you know about it?" he said, loud enough for everyone to hear.

I watched Kara's eyes as they darkened. "You're kidding," she gasped. "Who was it?"

Adonis shook his head. "Nobody knows. Isn't that right, Ser? Nobody knows who tried to kill our dear princess."

Jade stiffened, but the coy look on her face was unmoving.

"We're working on it," Serefin answered. Adonis stared at him for another second before saying, "I heard Malachi did quite the damage. There wasn't even a body to bury, was there?"

Serefin's jaw tightened.

Adonis moved his attention to Jade. "Did you see it?" he asked her. "Did you see him rip the head off the man's body? It's quite intense, really. Malachi has a gift." He eyed Jade, sizing her every reaction.

I wanted to rush to the table. I wanted to shut them all up.

But I also wanted to see how Jade acted when I wasn't around. Jade didn't have to like me. But she was my wife. I hoped that she had at least a tiny ounce of loyalty.

After all, I did save her life.

"He really does have a gift, doesn't he?" Jade added casually. "It's really no wonder he's going to be king. With all that power, he could take down any kingdom. Don't you agree?"

Every muscle in my body froze. I watched as Adonis stared at her, unblinking, like a stunned rabbit.

Kara's jaw was wide, and the rest of my brothers were too busy snickering to pay any attention.

"You seem to know a lot about my attack," she added. She leaned over the wooden table, propping her chin on her elbows. "Careful, brother. You don't want to get yourself into any trouble," she said with a wink.

Serefin choked next to her.

"It's been a while since we've seen you," Kara interjected, cutting the tension in the room. "I suppose that's your husband's doing?"

"Malachi and I have been very busy," Jade said. *Busy.* The way she said it made my blood crawl.

Kara smiled, but I knew her enough to know it was full of malice. "I'm sure you have," she said. "It's quite a shame, you know. I'm used to seeing so much more of him."

Jade smiled, but Serefin leaned in and whispered something in her ear. Whatever he said made her brows furrow.

"I suppose we'll have to learn to share," Kara said quietly.

Jade ignored Serefin's ongoing warnings and snapped her head to Kara.

"It's really a shame that my husband chose a human over a fae. That must be really hard for you, Kara. I sympathize with you, truly."

Kara growled, but my stomach flipped.

Jade was jealous.

And I liked it.

"Have your fun while it lasts, princess. It doesn't matter how deep you pierce your claws into him. He'll always be one of us."

Serefin was whispering to Jade again, and I saw him motioning to leave.

As if my wife had to go back to her room and hide from all of this.

I took a deep breath. Like I said, I was tired of people touching my things.

My feet didn't make a sound as I approached. In fact, nobody noticed me until I was standing directly behind Jade.

"I see I've been missing out on all the fun," I announced.

Kara stiffened, but my brothers didn't move an inch.

"Prince Malachi," Serefin greeted. "We were just leaving." He stood from his chair and moved to help Jade to the same.

"No need," I replied. "Jade has hardly eaten. I'm sure she'd like to enjoy the rest of her dinner. Right, Jade?"

I picked up a piece of her long hair and let it fall through my fingers. Her throat bobbed as she swallowed, but she didn't look at me.

"Right," she answered.

"Perfect," I said, taking Serefin's seat next to her.

Kara moved as if she, too, were about to leave. My brothers followed.

"Stop," I yelled. "Everyone can sit here until my wife is done eating."

My brothers laughed. "Yeah, we're not doing that," Lucien sneered. This won a laugh from Kara.

As much as I hated hurting my brothers, there was a power in me that was hungry for more. It was always there, always waiting to be unleashed.

Perhaps I would give it a small taste.

I blinked at Lucien, envisioning a black tendril of smoke circling his chest and tightening.

Lucien dropped to his knees, gasping for air.

I cleared my vision, taking a deep breath as the hunger for power subsided. A taste was all it needed.

And it was enough to keep the others from leaving the table.

Lucien scrambled back to his seat.

"You're a coward for that," he said through gritted teeth. I laughed. We all knew I could kill them all right here if I wanted to. We all knew the type of power I had access to, the type of power they would never wield.

Jade stared across the table at Lucien with a straight face, but I saw a small glisten of amusement in her eyes.

I didn't stop the smile that spread across my face.

"So where were we? Talking about me, weren't you?" I asked.

Kara spoke next. "Only that we heard about the attack on Jade. It's terrible news, Malachi. If there's anything we can do to help you, please just ask."

She placed a hand on my shoulder, and Jade's eyes followed it. She flinched, only for a second, before replacing her mask.

"That's very kind of you, Kara," she said. Something told me Jade had a lot of practice with shoving hatred aside, burning it deep down and replacing it with a facade.

I should know. I had been doing the same for decades.

I didn't move Kara's hand from my shoulder.

Instead, I placed my hand on Jade's thigh. It was a small movement, but I could feel the eyes of everyone. I could feel the amusement from my brothers and the annoyance from Kara.

But Jade didn't move.

At least she didn't flinch. That much was a relief.

Kara slowly moved her hand, placing it back in her lap. I left my hand on Jade's thigh as she picked up her fork.

"That's thoughtful of you, Kara, but Serefin and I have everything under control. Besides, I have reasons to suspect our attacker might be someone within our walls. But I'm sure you all know that by now."

"What makes you think that?" My brother Eli asked.

I eyed him carefully before answering, "A few different things. I don't see how someone could have gotten into the castle without being seen, for one."

"Surely the guards would have seen someone," Kara added.

"During the ceremony? There was so much going on, anyone could have snuck in," Adonis said.

I remembered how close Jade was to getting caught by them that night. They had wanted to meet up with her. They were trying to get her alone.

"You're right," I replied, keeping my composure. "Many things can happen in the chaos of the wedding ceremony. I'm only glad I was there to protect Jade from the threats this time."

I squeezed Jade's thigh lightly, and she dropped her fork.

"Sorry," she stammered. "It, uh, slipped."

I looked up to find Kara staring at my hand. And she was done hiding her emotions. "You should be more careful, Jade. One mistake will get you killed in Rewyth. Your husband should have warned you of that. Humans aren't supposed to be here."

Jade opened her mouth, but I spoke first. "Is that a threat, Kara?"

Kara knew better than to challenge me, but jealousy was a great motivator. "I'm just making sure Jade knows what she's getting into. If you're so worried about her safety, maybe she shouldn't be here."

I stood from the table. "Are you questioning my ability to keep Jade safe? Because I assure you, I am more than capable of eliminating any threat. *Any* threat."

Kara shook her head in disgust. "For a human?"

I motioned for Jade to stand next to me, and I wrapped an arm around her waist. "For my *wife*," I growled. "Let's go, Jade."

She nodded and followed me out of the room. I didn't let go of her until we were alone in the hallway. Surprisingly, she played along until we were alone, and shoved me away.

"This is your game now?" she hissed. "You ignore me for days then show up to be a possessive asshole?"

I held in my laughter. Jade looked wild. Her long, black hair was messy and unhinged. Her clothes hung awkwardly off her body, and her eyes seemed larger than the last time I had seen them.

Saints, I had missed her. I had actually *missed* her the past few days. Although I was never going to admit that.

"Possessive asshole?" I repeated. "You forget I am the next king. They should respect you more."

"I can handle myself, thanks," she replied.

"Oh really? You seemed to be doing a great job out there. Serefin shouldn't have let you leave."

"Because I'm your prisoner, right?" she asked. "I'm supposed to sit in my room like your property, and not leave until you tell me to? Is that right?"

I opened my mouth to reply, but couldn't speak. Yeah, that was right. That was exactly what I wanted from her. Because she wasn't safe here. Even my bedroom wasn't safe, but at least I knew where she was. At least I knew what she was doing.

"I can't risk you waltzing around the castle. You're a target."

She gave a 'who cares' motion with her arms, and let them fall to her sides. Her big eyes glistened, but the rest of her face was drenched in anger. "I don't want to be here," she said as she took a step closer to me. "I can't just sit in there and watch my life waste away."

My chest tightened, but I didn't budge. "It isn't safe, Jade." *I'm sorry*, I almost added. But I stopped myself. I wasn't sorry for protecting her. I wasn't sorry for wanting to keep her alive.

A single tear fell from her eye, but she didn't look away. "I want my life back," she said.

She was pleading with me. I knew that. This was probably the closest thing to begging that Jade would ever do.

But it didn't make a difference. I didn't care. Giving into her meant risking her life.

I opened my bedroom door and motioned for her to enter. Her jaw clenched and her nostrils flared. I knew she was holding back her emotion. Her mask was cracking. But hope was deadly in Rewyth, and Jade was holding onto a life she would never return to.

I leaned in close to her as I whispered in her ear, "What life, princess?"

And I shut the door, locking Jade in.

"I wasn't going to let them hurt her," Serefin said from behind me.

"I know you weren't."

He smiled. "Although you sure know how to put on a show."

"You think they had anything to do with this?" I asked him.

He shook his head. "I don't know, but they seem to know more than everyone else about the attack. And Kara's trouble. We both know that."

I agreed. "I'm only keeping her in here until I know she'll be safe," I explained. I don't know why I felt the need to explain myself to Serefin. He was never the type to question my decisions. He would follow me anywhere, he would do anything I asked him to do.

But still. Something in his expression made me continue, "As soon as I find out who's trying to kill her, she'll be free to roam the castle."

"I know, brother," Ser replied. "I get it."

I nodded and started to walk away.

"You can't keep her safe from everything," he yelled after me. "A human will always be a target in Rewyth. As much as we wish that weren't true."

I didn't turn around. I didn't acknowledge his words.

But Saints. He was right. I knew he was right. Jade had a lot to learn if she was going to survive in Rewyth.

CHAPTER 13
Jade

Two hundred days went by.

Okay, it was only four days. But it felt like two hundred.

The water couldn't get my skin clean enough. I stayed under the steam until I was sure I was going to melt away and float into the river myself. But it didn't matter how many times I shampooed my hair or how hard I scrubbed my skin, I couldn't forget the feeling of Malachi touching my thigh.

Holding my waist

Leaning in close.

I shook my head. It was ridiculous. It was *pathetic*.

My brain even restored to dreaming about him. As if I needed to think about him any more than I already had.

My thoughts were interrupted by a knock on the bathroom door.

"Go away, Malachi," I yelled.

But it wasn't Malachi who entered anyway, chirping herself on the ledge of the sink.

It was Adeline.

"Adeline!" I shrieked. "What are you doing in here? I'm kind of naked right now!"

"Oh, please," she said, flipping her long hair over her shoulder. "Humans are so prude. Mal thought you might be losing your mind in here or something. You know if you stay under the water too long it causes wrinkles."

"I'm fine!" I yelled.

"Yeah, he also said you would say that. And he told me it probably wasn't true."

I cursed under my breath.

"Heard that," Adeline chirped.

These damn fae.

I stepped out of the water and wrapped myself in one of the pristinely white towels Malachi had. The fact that they weren't all already stained with blood was impressive.

"I'm really fine, Adeline. I don't need a babysitter."

She squinted her eyes. "You should be dead right now. And that cut still looks bad."

I looked in the steamy mirror and tried not to cringe. Right in the middle of my throat, a bright red cut was nearly halfway healed.

A reminder of how close my assassin had gotten to succeeding.

No wonder Malachi was so pissed.

"I'm alive, which is better than I could have asked for."

"Yeah, but we have to keep you alive. And your will to live is a slightly important factor there."

I rolled my eyes. "I'm not going to do anything stupid, Adeline. I already told Malachi I would listen to him from now on."

Adeline glanced toward the bathroom door before hopping off the counter and stepping closer to me. "Mal can be...possessive. He doesn't like that someone laid a hand on you, Jade. And this is the first time he's been able to make some headway on whoever has been killing his wives. He's going to protect you no matter what. You understand that, don't you?"

I let my head rest on the wall behind me. "I'm willing to do whatever it takes to stay alive. If that means living, acting and breathing like a damn faerie, then so be it. But I can't stay locked up like this. I can't just sit in here like I'm nothing. I can protect myself."

I realized after I said the words that they may have been stupid, but when I looked to Adeline, she had a giant grin on her face.

"You have no idea how happy I am to hear that," she chirped, nearly jumping with excitement. "Now put these clothes on. I'm taking you somewhere."

I didn't have time to ask questions. Adeline was gone, leaving a stack of clothes on the counter.

After getting dressed, I had to admit I was impressed. Adeline hadn't picked out a ridiculous, revealing fae outfit. Instead, she brought me simple slacks and a basic tunic.

I could actually move freely. And I wasn't covered in blood or wearing Malachi's clothes.

Consider me grateful.

After a few minutes of walking, Adeline and I found ourselves leaving the castle and heading into the jungle-like woods that encapsulated the entire back half of the estate.

"Does Malachi know we're heading into the woods?" I asked Adeline.

She rolled her eyes and groaned. "What Mal doesn't know won't kill him. Besides, it can be really beautiful out here. He would just ruin it."

I followed her down a narrow stone path, the light around us slowly diminishing even though the sun had just fully risen.

She wasn't lying. The beauty of the castle should have been a huge indication as to how beautiful the jungle was going to be. Even so, the castle hardly compared. Thick vines weaved through massive trees, filling the space with a variety of greenery. Thick moss covered the stones we walked on, silencing every step we took further into the jungle. The sound of water pouring in the distance grew stronger and stronger as we continued.

I was about to tell Adeline to stop when we entered a clearing, revealing a small waterfall that was almost hidden in the vast stone structure behind it.

Hidden. Like it was here just for Adeline. Just for us.

"Saints," I mumbled. "This is what you dragged me out here for? It's gorgeous, Adeline."

She gave me a knowing smile and trotted forward, perching herself onto a bench-like structure I assumed she was responsible for.

"See!" She said. "It's not so terrible here, is it? You're a fighter, Jade. I knew that as soon as I met you. You're going to stick around, I just know it. So, you might as well not absolutely hate this place while you're here!"

I couldn't help but smile. This was undoubtedly the nicest thing anyone had done for me. Granted nobody ever did nice things for me at home, and all Adeline did was drag me into the jungle, but it was still true.

I couldn't believe it.

"I'm assuming this is where you hide while your brothers continue whatever feud they have going on."

"You have no idea, honey. I feel like I've spent years out here with all the fighting they do. But family is complicated. Mal knows that. I'm sure you'll learn about all of their silly politics soon enough."

Now it was my turn to groan. "I feel like I've learned enough already."

Adeline's eyes were full of pity when she looked at me. "I know this must be hard for you, Jade. You don't know who to trust and you don't know what to believe about us. After what happened..."

"It's really okay—"

"Mal can be terrifying. I could smell the blood the second I walked into that room, Jade, and that was after they had cleaned it all up. I've seen him kill. I've seen him slaughter people dozens of times. Just because I'm fae doesn't mean I'm heartless, despite what you humans may think."

I shoved her shoulder playfully, then she continued.

"This world can be daunting, and Malachi has been through a lot. He's had to turn into someone he doesn't want to be."

"He seemed pretty proud of himself after ripping that man's head off."

"For nearly killing you!" She said. "I would have done the same thing!"

I took a deep breath. This was all too much to process. I was starting to believe everything I had been told about Malachi, despite Adeline's confusing claims.

"How am I supposed to believe he'll protect me when he has the reputation that he has? I'm just a human. I'm nothing here."

"You're not nothing, Jade. You're Malachi's wife. That makes you untouchable."

"Well, his last wives were pretty touchable."

She gave me a look of pity. "This is going to be a never-ending cycle, Jade. The facts are that you're Mal's wife now, and you're also a Rewyth Princess."

"I'm not a princess," I mumbled.

"But you are. And you can either live here in fear every day, or you can do something about it. I know you're trying to help Mal find out who's been doing this. I don't have to tell you to be careful. You already know that."

I nodded, not sure of what else to say.

So I changed the subject. "Do you know Kara?" I asked.

Adeline groaned. "Please don't tell me she's bothering you. I've had enough of her to last me two lifetimes."

I smiled at her reaction. "She seems very attached to Malachi."

"Yeah, she has been for decades. Literally. Malachi had some fun with her, but it was never serious. Kara wants power. She's a snake, and we all know it. Even Malachi."

I scoffed. "I don't know. He seems to put up with her more than anyone else. If other people talked to him the way she does, they would be dead."

"I think Malachi feels bad for her. I do, anyway. She wasn't always this terrible. We actually used to be friends a long time ago."

"Really?" I asked. "You and Kara?"

Adeline nodded. "But that was before her obsession with my brother."

I thought about her words. "You don't think she would be killing Malachi's wives out of jealousy, do you?"

"The thought has crossed my mind, I'll admit. But Kara is harmless. She is jealous, yes. And you should avoid her at all costs. But she doesn't have it in her to actually kill someone out of cold blood."

I nodded. Adeline confirmed what I had been thinking. Kara was a spiteful brat, but I had known girls like her. They were all talk. Kara was used to getting her way, and I was an obstacle.

Although I can't say I liked the way she acted toward Malachi.

"Okay!" Adeline sighed. "Enough of this serious stuff. I brought you here to show you how beautiful faerie can be, so come on!"

She stood from the bench and kicked off her shoes.

"What are you doing?!" I yelled.

I was answered by the sound of her splashing into the water.

"What?" She yelled from the water. "It feels so nice!"

I laughed. It was a real laugh, and it somehow felt wrong, like I didn't deserve to be laughing.

Tessa was probably freaking out right now. For all she knew, I had been killed.

I had to go see her. Mal had to take me there.

And I had to help Malachi.

Adeline splashed a handful of water in my direction. "Are you jumping in or are you staying out there like a big baby?" She taunted.

I always loved swimming. Back home, I used to spend every morning swimming in the pond near our house.

But that was before I spent every day fighting for survival. For food. For Tessa.

That felt like ages ago.

But this was a new life. This was a new home. And as much as I hated to admit it, this was my new reality.

Adeline was right. Rewyth, as despicable as I might have thought it to be, did have a few benefits.

A gorgeous waterfall in the middle of the jungle was definitely one of them.

Adeline clapped her hands with excitement as a stood from the bench, kicking my own shoes off and jumping into the water.

The water was a welcoming, luxurious pool of bliss. Okay, maybe that was an exaggeration. But it was absolutely amazing.

I held my breath and dunked beneath the water, letting the weightlessness of my body drift.

"I knew you'd love it!" Adeline said a few feet away.

The water hardly covered my chest when I stood on the rocks that rested at the bottom.

"My sister would love it here," I said to her. "She usually hates the outdoors... but this..."

"Welcome to Rewyth, Princess Jade. This is just the beginning."

I opened my mouth to respond, to object to the princess title once more, but Adeline's eyes had settled on something behind me.

I didn't turn around. I froze as I heard what she was hearing.

Footsteps in the jungle headed straight toward us.

CHAPTER 14
Malachi

I was going to kill Adeline.

She had seriously taken Jade into the jungle? After what just happened? After I explicitly told her to keep an eye on her in my bedroom, not parade her around to the most dangerous part of Rewyth.

I normally trusted Adeline, but there were times when she acted like a stupid teenage girl. Part of me didn't blame her. Like the rest of us, her childhood had been ripped away from her. There was no time for fun and games in the royal family, and Adeline had always had a hard time making friends.

It was hard to know who you could trust when everyone in faerie was a greedy asshole who wanted something from you.

But I knew Adeline would like Jade, although I was surprised to learn Jade had been reciprocating those feelings.

No, I didn't care about what I had said to Jade last

night. I didn't care about the look on her face as I locked her into that room again. I shoved those thoughts aside. She was going to have to learn what she was up against, and if that meant making her hate me any more than she already did, then so be it.

If it meant keeping her alive.

If it meant figuring out who had tried to kill her.

It was worth it.

I had learned very little about the identity of our attackers. Kara and my brothers were gossips, but someone else in the castle had to know something. Had to have seen something.

Someone in this castle thought they could outsmart me. Thought they could kill my wife.

I just had to find out who was behind this, and I would throw a celebration around their deaths.

But it's not like I could go around asking questions. I couldn't trust anyone. Every single fae in this damned castle was a suspect in my eyes. Even family. Even guards.

I heard their voices and took a sharp turn, toward the lagoon. I should have guessed it. This had been Adeline's favorite spot since we were children.

The sound of laughter nearly made me pause. It was warm and full of life, something I wasn't used to.

Most people were cold around me. I didn't blame them.

When I stomped through the trees and into the clearing, I froze in my tracks.

And then Jade screamed.

A massive tiger, one that had likely been stalking them this whole time, lunged toward Jade. It splashed as its body hit the water, and they both went under.

Adeline yelled and threw herself toward Jade and the tiger.

I was already moving.

The next few moments were a blur of water, blood, screaming, and limbs flailing in the lagoon.

I gripped the tiger from behind and threw myself backward, taking it with me.

Jade gasped as she resurfaced, but the tiger thrashed in my arms.

"Adeline!" I yelled. "Get her out of here!"

Adeline moved toward Jade, but so did the tiger.

It was too slippery. The massive animal twisted from my grasp.

But Adeline was there. She had her hands around the tiger in an instant, stopping it in its tracks. She screamed as she fought, squeezing hard on its large neck.

The tiger whimpered. I moved to help Adeline, and together we threw it from the pond.

Its wet body landed on the ground, but it wasn't dead.

Not yet.

The tiger stood and looked at us. For a moment, I thought it was going to lunge again. I regained control and pictured black smoke surrounding us, protecting us from the tiger.

Jade couldn't see it. Adeline couldn't see it. But animals had always been able to see my power.

The tiger shook its head and backed away before darting back into the jungle.

All three of us stood in the shoulder-deep water, panting.

I was the first one to speak. "I hope you both have a very good explanation for this."

My sister swallowed. "I'm sorry Mal, I was just trying to–"

"Stop," I interrupted. "I don't want your apology right now. You both would be dead right now if I hadn't come looking for you."

"I would have stopped it!" Adeline argued.

"Really?" I asked. "You really think you're in the position to fight off a grown tiger that's likely twice your size, all while protecting Jade at the same time?"

Adeline stammered, looking for her next words. But Jade interrupted. "She was trying to help me, Malachi."

"And what exactly was she helping you with? You're this desperate to get yourself killed?"

"She was trying to get me out of that prison," Jade replied. Her voice shook, likely from the adrenaline of what just happened, but she still held her chin high. "It's not our fault there was a massive animal waiting to attack us out here. How were we supposed to know that?"

"You and I will talk about this later," I said to Adeline. "Let's go, Jade."

The girls looked at each other and Jade scoffed before the three of us crawled out of the lagoon. Jade's breaths were still coming out in short bursts.

"I trusted you, Adeline," I said quietly.

She lowered her head. "I know. I'm sorry. I'm sorry, Jade."

Jade grabbed Adeline's hand. "Don't apologize. Thank you for bringing me here. It really is gorgeous."

Adeline looked up and smiled shyly before walking back to the castle, leaving Jade and I alone.

CHAPTER 15
Jade

Malachi didn't say a single word to me as we walked back through the jungle toward the castle.

And the way he had spoken to Adeline...

He had crushed her. I could see the way Adeline physically shrank at the way he didn't trust her. At the way he ridiculed her. Adeline had looked up to him, had tried to help me, had made me laugh for the first time in what seemed like decades, and he had put her down because of it.

Like I said. *Ignorant bastard.*

Once I was certain my voice wasn't going to shake, I spoke up. "She was just trying to help me," I said as we approached the large castle. My stomach dropped at the sight of it, like my body knew I wouldn't be leaving again anytime soon.

Malachi shook his head in front of me. He hadn't released the tension in his fists for the entire time we had been walking, and his muscles had been flexing nonstop under his thin shirt that was now plastered to his body with water.

Not like I had been looking.

"She knows better than to disobey me," he growled without turning to face me.

The words alone were enough to make me laugh out loud. "Okay, *father*," I spat. I was playing with fire, but I didn't care. Malachi had made it very clear that he could kill anyone he wanted to, yet here I was. Alive.

Malachi stopped walking so abruptly, I almost bumped into his back.

When he turned to face me, his eyes were swarming with emotion.

"Don't ever talk to me like that," he said, pointing a finger at my chest. "And don't pretend like you know anything about my family or what goes on here. You know nothing about this court, and you know nothing about me."

"Because you won't tell me anything," I pushed. "And you've been ignoring me for days!"

He laughed, but it chilled me to my bones. I crossed my arms over my chest and tried not to shiver. "If you knew everything, you would run like the Saints as far as you could to get away from here. So don't ask for something you can't handle, princess."

I debated his words for a second. He had turned and continued walking, but as I followed after him, I added, "I want to learn how to fight."

"To fight?"

"I want to learn how to protect myself," I said, trying and failing to keep my voice from breaking. "I don't want to be afraid. I want to have a fighting chance at survival. You made it very clear that I'm as good as useless here."

He hesitated, and for the second time today I thought he was going to apologize, but he didn't.

"Fine," he said after a few awkward seconds. "I think we could all benefit from you knowing how to protect yourself against the fae."

The fae. He said the words as if he wasn't one himself. I nodded in response but said nothing else. The conversation was over.

I followed him as he entered the castle, completely ignoring everyone who seemed to be gawking at him. I copied his movements, keeping my head down as we weaved through the maze of the hallways.

Something on my leg was burning, but I didn't dare to look. Adrenaline had been pulsing through my body since the tiger had attacked, and I hadn't thought to check if I had been injured in the crossfire.

I certainly wasn't going to check in front of Malachi. He didn't need any more reason to keep me locked away.

I was still dripping wet. My hair was leaving a trail of water on the white flooring, but Malachi didn't seem to notice. Or care.

Probably the latter.

Malachi turned another corner and tensed immediately.

I lifted my head for the first time since we entered the castle, only to be standing in front of the King of Rewyth himself, and all five of his sons.

CHAPTER 16
Malachi

I wanted to grab Jade and drag her back into my bedroom, where I could lock my door and keep her there, away from the monstrosities of my family.

But it was too late. I had successfully avoided the bastards since our discussion the other day, and now it was time to confront them.

My father and my brothers stood just a few feet away, every single pair of eyes fell on me.

And then I watched as every single pair of eyes shifted to the dripping wet girl standing behind me.

My *wife*.

"Well, well, well," my father said, stepping forward. "The lovely prince and princess. It's quite a pleasure to see you doing so well!"

He meant *alive*. It was a pleasure to see Jade alive.

I wasn't buying it. "We were just heading back to my quarters," I said as I reached a hand back to Jade.

She grabbed it without hesitating, which nearly made me sigh in relief after the fight we just had.

Smart girl.

I wondered if she could feel how tense I was. How important it was for her to play along here.

My father eyed us both up and down, lingering his gaze on Jade's wet clothes for a few seconds too long before saying, "I'm calling a court meeting this evening. I suggest you attend and bring your new...wife."

The way he said it had me clenching my jaw, but I plastered a smile on my face. "I'll see if I can fit it in," I said through gritted teeth. Jade kept her mouth shut beside me, which was surprising. Especially as my father kept staring at her.

"Anything else?" I said after a few moments of silence. Adonis whispered something to Lucien and they both laughed. I felt my composure crumbling. "Care to share with the group?" I pushed.

I couldn't help it. After what happened with Jade last night, I wasn't taking anyone's bullshit. People had been pushing me to the limits for far too long.

Perhaps they had forgotten why I was called the Prince of Shadows.

Adonis squared his shoulders before responding, "Oh we were just admiring your wife's appropriate court attire. I supposed none of us prepared for her to be around long enough to need her own tailor, right?"

They laughed again.

The power building in my body was almost enough to become tangible. They knew who they were messing with.

They knew what the consequences would be. I snarled at him before my father held up a hand. "Enough, Malachi," he said, sounding bored as ever. Was he serious? They talk about my wife, the princess of Rewyth that way, and he takes their side? "I'm tired of these immature games you all play. We'll see you this evening for the court meeting. We can discuss the politics of this arrangement then."

He didn't look at us again as he walked by, sauntering out of the hallway with his posse of princes in trail.

Jade exhaled loudly as soon as we were alone in the hallway. "Shit," she mumbled, crossing her arms over her body once more. "No offense, but your family is a bunch of assholes."

I smiled quickly before the realization of the situation hit me.

Jade had actually survived her first few nights in Rewyth. And now she was going to have to survive a court meeting. This might be an even more difficult task than the first.

"Let's go," I said, guiding her back down the hallway toward my room. "Things are about to get very interesting."

"Because they were so boring already," she mumbled under her breath.

I clenched my fists. "You realize fae can hear every dumb thing you mumble under your breath, right?"

Jade just smiled and flipped her wet hair over her shoulder. "Good, you were meant to."

She strutted past me and continued walking to my bedroom.

Our bedroom.

Did she not understand how serious this was? Did she not know the dangers of the situation she was about to be in?

I followed her in and shut the door behind me. Jade just perched herself on the sofa, completely ignoring the fact that her hair was still dripping water.

"We need to talk," I said, pacing past her and examining. "I need you to do everything I tell you to do tonight."

Jade tensed, but kept her calm expression. "For the court meeting?"

"Yep."

"Do you think someone there wants me dead?"

Her face was blank.

"I don't know."

Silence.

It was only a couple seconds but it felt like hours.

"Okay," she said finally. "What do you need me to do?"

I did a double take, definitely did not expect her to say that. But I was relieved nonetheless.

I leaned against the wall as I gathered my thoughts. What did I need her to do? Saints, I had no idea. The wedding was bad enough, and we had barely survived that. This was something different. The public eye wasn't here to keep my family's behavior in line. These

145

court meetings got ugly, and few of them ended without any bloodshed.

Whether it's from my idiot brothers punching each other or worse.

"First, you'll need new clothes. Court clothes. I'll have Adeline bring some for you."

She nodded.

"And you'll have to stay quiet. Actually quiet this time. My brothers will.... They'll try to start something. They always do. There's no telling what they have in mind, considering there's never been a wife at any of these meetings."

"None of your brothers are married?"

"Nope. Apparently I'm the only one my father hates enough for that."

She cringed at my words, and I immediately wanted to take them back.

But Jade just lifted her chin and said, "I guess that makes two of us, then."

I met her eyes from across the room. Jade had been a surprise, indeed. The fact that she hated the fae so much, but still wanted to defend Adeline, said everything I needed to know about her. Jade had a soft spot underneath her badass, rock solid demeanor.

But in Rewyth, that was as good as a death sentence.

Show no weakness. Yield no mercy.

"You know how to use that thing, right?" I asked her regarding her knife. I assumed she could wield a weapon, but in the two times she had been attacked here in Rewyth, she hadn't used it.

Something dark hardened her expression.

"I've used it before," she said. I fought the urge to ask her when.

"Good," I said, pulling an iron knife of my own from my hip. "Because fae are strong. Much stronger than any human. And you've seen the animals in the jungle now. That tiger was the least of your worries out there. You have to be ready."

"For what, exactly? For your father to try and kill me? Sorry, but I'm not sure I'd have any chance against that. Dagger or not."

"Let me show you," I said as I pushed myself away from the wall. I didn't think, just acted.

She stood up slowly, but fear crept into her features. I know she was thinking about how I held the knife to her throat, and probably how the assassin had done the same hours earlier.

"Relax," I said. "I'm not going to hurt you."

She snapped her gaze to me. "Great, it's so nice to know my husband isn't going to kill me, despite how much he likes threatening everyone else."

My breath stalled.

"I didn't mean to scare you," I said. I wasn't sure which incident I was even talking about.

She simply nodded. "This is my new life, isn't it? Fight to survive?"

"You're human, Jade. Hasn't it always been that way?"

She stiffened again. "Just because I'm not fae, just because I don't live in a fancy castle or party with rich court members every day, doesn't mean I've been fighting for survival every day."

I considered her words. "When I saw you in the forest, I could have guessed differently."

"I was fighting for my family."

"Quite a family you have."

"Likewise."

I froze. Jade stared me down. Her and I were different. I knew that. Jade was a human who was living off scraps, hunting her own food.

I was a prince of Rewyth. In fact, I was the most feared prince in the kingdom. And it wasn't for no reason.

But Jade didn't need to know that just yet.

I held the knife to my side, pushing the thoughts aside. "The quickest way to harm a fae is a silver blade to the heart. It might not kill them, but it will hurt them enough for you to run and get help."

She held her own knife, examining it as if it were the only thing keeping her from death.

"Try to stab me," I said.

"What?"

"You heard me."

"I'm not going to stab you," she sneered.

"No," I agreed. "You're not. But you can try."

Her brows furrowed. "Are all fae as cocky as you?"

I smirked. I couldn't help it. "Not all fae are the heir to the kingdom."

"And not all fae are the Prince of Shadows."

"Also correct," I said.

Jade's hair was beginning to dry, curling slightly at the ends where the long locks hit her waist. She was thin, thinner than she was in the forest the first time I had seen her.

She wasn't strong enough to fight off a fae.

As if she could read my thoughts, Jade lunched forward, dagger in hand and aimed directly at my chest.

Her form was decent, but I easily batted her away with my hand.

"Try again."

She huffed, clenching her fists. It was good if she was getting angry. Anger would give her strength. Adrenaline.

She lunged again, this time with a grunt of frustration.

I grabbed her arm and twisted. Her weapon clattered to the floor.

"Are you even trying?" I asked.

She backed away and ran her hands over her face. "This is stupid. I'm not fast enough."

"You have to be, Jade. And if you can't be faster, you have to be smarter."

"Smarter than who, exactly? The dozens of fae who may or may not want me dead?"

I rolled my eyes. She might not have been trying to be difficult, but we were stuck in an endless cycle.

"Are you done feeling sorry for yourself?" I asked.

"Excuse me?"

"Look," I said. "I get that you're in a shit situation. But your attitude really isn't helping."

"My attitude?" she repeated. I just nodded in response. "I'm sorry that I can't be happy and helpful all the time when my sister might be freaking out, your brothers may want to kill me, you ripped off someone's head on our wedding night, and now we might be walking into some sort of testosterone bomb. Apologies, my prince."

I chose my next words carefully. "You know that's not what I meant."

She just nodded, the tough walls of her composure slowly crumbling behind her deep eyes. Part of me wanted to comfort her, but I didn't.

"You have no idea what it's like," she said. "None of you do. You don't know what it's like to starve for days because your father was too drunk to come home and bring food. And when he finally showed up, he had spent the rest of our money on drinking. You don't know how it feels to have to hunt and steal for food just so your little sister doesn't starve. And you certainly don't know what it feels like to have your coward of a father ship you to the fae because he can't pay his own debt. So, I think the next time you have an opinion on my attitude, or anything about me for that matter, you can respectfully shove it."

I just nodded. "Okay."

She looked shocked, like she expected me to fight back. "Okay," she repeated, picking up the dagger. "So teach me how to use this."

"I thought you said you've used it before. On men, if I'm not mistaken," I said, repeating her words from the first night I met her.

A wicked smile spread across her face. One that almost made me smile in response. "Stories for another time, husband. I need to know how to use this against the fae."

I nodded. We would definitely have to come back to that. "The facts are that you won't be stronger or faster than a fae. Probably ever. So you'll have to use other advantages."

"Like what?"

"You're human. Nobody's going to expect you to fight back. Surprise is going to be your best bet. Just keep that thing where you can grab it easily, somewhere nobody is going to see it."

"You had a pretty easy time knowing I had this at the wedding."

"Maybe, but nobody else should be looking at you that closely." Jade blushed, but I didn't back down. Something primal inside of me wouldn't allow it.

"Your brother seemed to be looking just as closely as you," she said, a smirk on her face and a hand on her hip. She was taunting me.

I didn't stop the growl that rumbled in my chest. Jade's eyes only widened. "Does that bother you?"

She held my gaze, testing me. She was brave, that much was certain. But I had already told her I wouldn't hurt her.

Maybe she was getting too confident.

In one second, I grabbed her around her waist and hurled her against the wall, pinning her there with my arms.

"I could kill you right now," I growled.

She lifted her chin in silent defiance. "Then why don't you?" she whispered.

The feeling of her breath on my cheek made me shiver. I held her there for a few more seconds, pressing her body against the wall, staring into her eyes. She wasn't going to back away. She knew I wouldn't kill her, and she was too damn stubborn to admit she was wrong.

Saints. This girl was going to get me killed.

The sharp, copper smell of blood distracted me. "Are you bleeding?" I asked, backing away from the wall and looking her up and down.

Jade took a deep breath and looked down at her leg. Her trousers were black, but I could now see the thick coat of blood that covered them, dripping down to the floor.

How had I not noticed that before?

"It's not that bad," she mumbled. "I can barely even feel it."

"That's because you're stubborn," I replied. I didn't wait for Jade to protest. I put an arm under her knees and picked her up, carrying her to the bed.

"It's seriously fine!" she said as I knelt before her and rolled up her pant leg.

Jade hissed in pain. "You should have told me you were hurt," I whispered.

I grabbed my shirt and ripped a strip of fabric from the bottom.

Jade went still as my fingers traced up her leg, just above her knee, where the slice of a claw began.

"You shouldn't have been out there," I whispered. She didn't respond. I began tying the fabric over her wound, aware of every single time my skin brushed against hers.

Jade was silent. When I finished tying the knot, I looked up at her. And I immediately wished I hadn't.

She was staring at me with the same longing that I was feeling. The same longing that neither of us could act on.

My hand lingered under her calf. I slid it up, just an inch, and waited for Jade's reaction.

She inhaled sharply, as if my touch affected her just as badly as hers affected me.

"I should get ready for the court meeting," she insisted.

I cleared my throat.

"Right," I said. I stood up and backed away from the bed. "Of course."

"But thank you, Malachi. And thank you for saving my life today. Again."

"Anytime," I replied. Jade smiled at me before heading to the bathroom, leaving me alone in the bedroom.

CHAPTER 17
Jade

"How does it look?" I asked Malachi. He was standing in the corner of the room, his massive black wings tucked behind each shoulder blade. He had changed into a sleek black t-shirt and jeans, which matched his wings and his hair.

A Prince of Shadows, indeed.

"You look fine," he said, although I could tell he didn't even bother glancing at me. Since our encounter earlier, he had been ignoring me completely.

But maybe that was for the best.

I had let myself forget who Malachi really was. I had let myself fall for his soft touch on my leg.

Saints, I had nearly *kissed* him.

Malachi might have been my husband, but he was still fae. And I was still trying to survive.

I looked at myself in the mirror, smoothing down my black corset and matching skirt that fell past my feet. "How the saints am I supposed to fight off an attacker in a skirt like this?"

His shoulders shook in laughter in the mirror's reflection, but he still didn't meet my gaze. "Your five minutes of training won't help much anyway, princess."

Jackass.

The nerves in my stomach were enough to make me want to vomit, but I didn't dare tell Malachi that.

Show no weakness, as he said. Yield no mercy.

These fae weren't about to see me cower.

I took a deep breath and let go of the nerves. I was a survivor. A fighter. "Let's get this over with," I said, turning from the mirror.

Malachi looked up for the first time since I got dressed. His expression was blank, which made me more nervous than if he were pissed off. "Don't forget what I told you," he said in a low voice. "Keep quiet."

Warning laced every word. I just nodded.

He looked at me, eyes finally moving from my face, landing on my new dress. I had never worn something like this. My gown at the wedding had been a singular piece of fabric that flowed with my body. This dress was thick and structured, and I couldn't take a deep breath without my chest nearly spilling from the top.

He opened his mouth like he was about to say something, but we were both interrupted when the bedroom door creaked open.

Serefin.

"I'm here to escort you, my lord," he said in an

unusually polite voice. Malachi nodded, as if the two of them had done this dozens of times before.

Whatever softness had lingered in his gaze disappeared. "Let's go, Jade," he said in a voice that was rumbling with power. He didn't wait to see if I followed him before storming out of the room and into the hallway.

"You look beautiful," Serefin whispered to me as I forced my feet to move. "Don't worry. Everything will be fine."

Was he talking to himself? Or me?

I didn't dare to ask. Just kept my mouth shut as Serefin guided me behind Malachi, his prince and my husband, the heavy pit of dread in my stomach growing with every step.

Malachi

The scent of Jade's fear was about to rip me apart. She knew just as well as I did that if the people in this room wanted her dead, they just might be able to succeed.

Every ounce of my body was on alert. I wasn't going to let anything surprise me. Prepare for the worst, always prepare for the worst.

For all I knew, we were walking into a death trap.

I couldn't even look at her, but I heard her and Serefin's footsteps echoing behind me until we were standing right outside of the solar. I could hear the voices of the others already inside.

We were the last to arrive.

I closed my eyes and took a deep breath. It wasn't going to happen again. I was going to protect her.

I had to.

Without thinking, I slipped my hand into Jade's. We had to appear united in front of the court. We had to at least pretend to act like a couple.

Jade just stood next to me, a quick flash of shock on her face before she covered it up. Burying it deep down where it couldn't hurt her.

Good. She couldn't afford to feel anything. Neither could I.

I balled my free hand into a fist, nearly piercing the skin on my palm. Serefin nodded at me once before pushing open the doors.

My brothers were seated in the center of the room, around my father. They didn't even glance at us as we walked inside.

Ignorant bastards.

The other members of the court, however, weren't as obtuse.

"The man of the hour," Carlyle said to me, walking forward and holding out his hand.

I smiled in relief. "Isn't it past your bedtime, old man?" He laughed before turning his attention to Jade.

"And I believe congratulations are in order. It's a pleasure to have you in this court, Lady Farrow," he said, bending down to kiss her knuckles.

He was always such a flirt. If he wasn't triple my age, I might have kicked his ass for it.

But Carlyle had always been good to me. He had pure intentions, which was a rarity for the fae, I had to admit.

It was decades ago when I met him. My father had sent me as a last straw during a war between our countries. He had sent me as a weapon, but I had returned as Carlyle's ally.

And friend.

A dull ache threatened my chest, but I cleared my throat and buried that memory.

Jade was doing her best to look confident, but she was clearly out of her element, staring at Carlyle like he was some sort of Saint.

"Thank you," she finally responded to Carlyle. "Although I can't say everyone has been as welcoming as you."

She better watch it. Everything we said would be heard by dozens of ears. Ears that would pay millions to watch me burn.

To watch *us* burn.

And what better way to watch a man suffer than to torture his wife?

No. They didn't know I cared about her. Saints, I *didn't* care about her. But they had to believe that, too. At least here.

"Shall we?" I said, guiding Jade with a hand on her back. We maneuvered through the sea of whispering fae and found our seats at the head of the table.

Right next to my father.

I simply nodded at him, not trusting my own mouth to not say something stupid.

"Princess Jade," Adonis said. "You're looking well. It's a pleasure to see you again so soon."

A feral growl filled the room, and it took me a second to realize it was from me.

Adonis looked at me as if I were unhinged.

Maybe I was.

"What?" he asked. "Am I not allowed to speak to your wife?"

Jade opened her mouth like she was going to answer for herself, but I cut her off. "This is a court meeting, and Jade knows nothing of the court, so it's best if you don't address her at all today. She already has enough to think about. Right, Jade?"

Anger pulsed through my body with every heartbeat.

"As a matter of fact," I said to the room, very aware of my father sitting just feet away from me, "nobody in this room speaks to Jade. If you would like to address something, you can speak to me about it."

The twins snickered before one of them, Eli, said, "well what if we want to tell her that she looks expensive? How much are human whores worth these days anyway?" He asked, hardly containing his laughter.

Jade stiffened. The room silenced.

That was all I needed.

I didn't draw my sword. I didn't need it. My black

wings casted a shadow around me as I stepped forward toward my brother.

His face straightened. He had never seen me this way before. Most of them hadn't.

This was the Prince of Shadows everyone talked about. This was the prince that was a weapon to Rewyth.

The ground began to rumble. "Control yourself, Malachi," my father warned, but I pushed his words aside. I kept my focus on Eli, on the words he said.

I didn't care if it hurt Jade, but disrespect to Jade was disrespect to me.

Perhaps they had forgotten. I was going to make them remember.

Power rumbled through the air. *My* power. The same power that could kill with a single thought. The same power that made the entire kingdom fear me. That made my father use me as a weapon all this time.

I wasn't planning on killing my brother, but I would scare him just enough. He would be the example of what would happen if anyone messed with Jade again.

"Mal, stop," Jade's voice cut through the air. Normally I would have ignored it, but her voice was strained. The tiniest smell of fear filled the air.

It was enough to stop me in my tracks, to stop any amount of power that was building up inside of me.

I blinked a few times, now very aware of the fact that I had pinned my brother against the wall, arm against his neck hard enough that he was fighting to breathe.

I dropped him and backed away.

The entire room was staring at me in awe. Including my father. Including Jade.

"Malachi," my father boomed from his chair. "Are you able to keep your temper intact? Or must we excuse you from this court meeting?"

I clenched my fists. "I'll be fine." One look at Eli, who was now cowering against the wall, told me he was done with his snide comments.

And everyone else was now too stunned to speak.

"Very well, then," my father announced to the room. "Now that the drama has subsided, it's best we go ahead and get started. Everyone take your seats."

We all did as we were told. Jade ended up sitting between myself and Lucien, who apparently was having a hard time keeping his eyes off of her.

I made a mental note to teach him a lesson later, as well.

Part of me wanted to lean to Jade and ask her if she was okay. I wanted to tell her she didn't need to be afraid of me, and that I wasn't going to let people speak about her that way.

But not now. Not in front of a room full of fae who were looking for weaknesses in me.

Certainly not in front of my father.

My father cleared his throat with a sound that made me want to gag. "We have a few topics to discuss today," he started, "but I would like to begin by welcoming our dear princess, Jade Farrow, to the meeting today." Jade stiffened next to me, but she forced a small smile onto her face. "Jade's role as Malachi's wife will serve Rewyth in many ways, the first and foremost to unite the human and fae lands once and for all."

I blinked. What was he talking about?

"How is a human supposed to unite our lands?" One of the elders asked. The elders were usually the ones to voice concern during our court meetings, especially when something was changing. Having a human in this room was the biggest change of all. "She can hardly be in a room of fae without reeking of fear. No offense intended, dear," he said.

I glanced at Jade, half expecting some sort of sassy retort. But her expression was unchanging, as if the man's words did nothing but bore her.

"Your concerns are something we have thought long and hard about," my father responded. I nearly laughed out loud. How ridiculous was that? My father hardly thought about any humans, let alone bringing peace to their lands. "It is no secret that the humans and the fae have been in a feud for centuries, but for what? What started as a petty war years and years ago has now led the humans to famine and poverty. They're starving to death every day, and our dear princess here can attest to that."

Dozens of eyes turned to my wife. She blinked a few times, as if she were just processing what my father had said.

I took a deep breath and said, "What specifically are you hoping to achieve from this union, father?"

He turned to me with a smile big enough to show his rotting teeth. "Thank you for asking, son. This brings me to our first agenda item today." I stiffened, bracing for his next words. I sensed Jade doing the same. "You and your wife are being sent to govern your own lands, where fae and humans will live together in one place."

The room erupted in chaos.

CHAPTER 18

Jade

My ears were ringing, but that didn't stop me from hearing the stream of profanity that left Malachi's mouth as he stood from the chair.

"Everyone calm down!" the King yelled. His voice was barely audible over the crowd of fae yelling questions of their own.

"And when were you planning on sharing this plan with me, father?" Malachi asked. His face was red, and I wondered if it was from anger or embarrassment.

"I'm sharing it with you now," his father boomed. "Now sit down."

Malachi huffed and, to my surprise, sat back down in his chair.

I guess the beast could be controlled, after all.

After a few seconds, the room began to silence, all eyes locked on the King.

Including mine.

"This has been a plan of mine for quite some time," he started. "And it is in Rewyth's best interests to eventually unite the humans and the fae."

"Why?" Someone shouted. "What could we possibly want from them?"

As much as I hated to admit it, I was actually thinking the same thing. The fae lived in wealth and riches in Rewyth. And the humans? We were scum. We were poor and sick. We had nothing.

We had nothing to give the fae.

Which means the King had something else in mind.

Malachi must have realized that too. His eyes filled with anger, curiosity and stubbornness as he stared at his father.

"The humans have something we don't have. They may be poor. They may be sick. They may be disgusting creatures that can't take care of themselves..."

I rolled my eyes.

"...but they have safety."

Now it was my turn to look confused. What could he possibly be talking about? Compared to the fae, humans were the furthest thing from safe. We didn't have to worry about our enemies, because we were too busy worried about if we were going to starve to death or not.

"He's talking about Trithen," Malachi mumbled to himself, just loud enough for me to hear.

Trithen...it sounded familiar.

"Because of the old treaties between the fae and the

human lands, the fae are forbidden to attack any lands where humans reside. Or they risk punishment from the Paragon."

The room collectively began absorbing his words, some even nodding along.

I wanted to ask Malachi what the Saints they were talking about, but I resisted, biting the inside of my cheek as he continued.

The King stood up and began pacing the room. "The humans, however, conveniently reside in the land that is separating Rewyth from our sister kingdom, Fearford."

Adonis was the one who spoke next. "So, you think the Paragon will allow you to move fae into the human lands? Won't there be riots?"

"Not if we do this correctly. You see, this union proves that fae and humans can live peacefully together. Especially when the new prince and princess are madly in love."

"The humans won't accept this," Malachi added.

"They will if we stop them from starving. We'll share our resources in exchange for sharing their land."

I couldn't believe what I was hearing. He actually wanted to make a deal with the humans?

"So, you'll give away our food and money for a chance at posting some of our fae closer to Fearford?"

"Exactly."

The room erupted in a low murmur of voices.

I didn't realize Lucien leaning into my ear until he began whispering, "Better buckle up, sweetheart. The humans might not hate you yet, but they're sure about to."

"Shut up, Lucien," Malachi responded before I had the chance. My head was spinning. It was all too much information to absorb. I placed my elbows on the large wooden table and rested my head on my wrists, rubbing my temples lightly.

"Are you sure the princess is up for it?" A new voice yelled from the corner of the room. "She doesn't seem too fit for the challenge."

I couldn't stay quiet. I know Malachi had warned me, but I had to say something.

"What do you all know about the humans, anyway?" I said without lifting my head. "We starve. We beg. We suffer. You will never last in the human lands."

The entire room went silent. Even Malachi.

When I finally lifted my head, the King was the only one smiling. "You underestimate your own union, child," he said. "This is your duty. You and Malachi will make this happen. This is the sole purpose of this union, so it's in you and your family's best interests to make this happen. Do you understand?"

I forced myself to nod, but couldn't stop the way my teeth clenched and nostrils flared.

Malachi put a hand on my knee, likely to attempt to stop the rush of anger that was now bubbling to the surface.

His fingers tightened. I sat back in my chair.

"And why me? Why can't you have Adonis marry a human and move to Fearford?" Malachi asked.

This earned a snicker from Adonis, but Malachi shot him a death glare that almost made me shiver.

That shut Adonis up.

"You're the heir to the kingdom, Malachi. Who better than to unite our species?"

Malachi snorted, crossing his arms and leaning back in his chair.

Of course, nobody was going to ask my opinion on the matter. I was just the dumb human, along for the ride.

"Any questions?" The King asked. The room was silent. My heart was pounding in my chest, definitely loud enough for all of these annoying fae ears to hear. "Great," he said. "Then this meeting is over. Malachi, prepare to move to Fearford by the end of the week."

I could barely stand as I followed Malachi out of the room. I half-begged my body to hold it together, to wait until we were alone to have a meltdown.

Malachi and I were being sent away to rule human lands. I hadn't decided if this was a death sentence, or the best thing that had happened since I married the Prince of Shadows.

CHAPTER 19
Malachi

Jade hadn't spoken since we left the court meeting. I made sure to get her out of there as fast as possible once it was over, but she still hadn't said a word.

It was concerning.

"You understand what this means, right?" I said after a few minutes of silence. Jade had laid on the bed, staring into the ceiling above her. Completely emotionless.

"I understand," was all she replied.

Her silence was killing me. Couldn't she be angry? Couldn't she come up with some snarky comment or bash my father for such a dumb idea?

Jade sat up, supporting herself on her elbow as she finally looked me in the eyes. "I want to go home," she said.

"Okay," I said carefully. "Once we get to Fearford it should be easy to–"

"No," she interrupted. "Tonight. I want you to take me home tonight."

"Tonight?" I repeated. The sun was already down. Leaving Rewyth and crossing into the human lands would take weeks of planning, maybe more. Especially without my father knowing. "That's impossible, Jade. We can't just leave."

She stared at me, not even blinking. Not a flicker of emotion crossed her features. Had her cheekbones gotten sharper since she had been here? "Tonight," she demanded. "Or I won't go to Fearford with you."

I didn't stop myself from laughing that time. "You think you have a choice, princess? Do you think either of us have a choice?"

She dropped herself from her elbows and fell back on the bed. I stayed where I was with my back against the wall.

"I'm not trying to be an ass," I said as I attempted to quiet my voice.

"Could have fooled me," she mumbled. Whatever fiery spirit she had keeping her emotions locked in was slowly deteriorating. Melancholy began swimming in her features, leaking into her voice.

Saints. I couldn't believe I was actually considering this.

"We can attempt it," I said. "But a single ounce of trouble, and we turn around."

She sat up, head snapping in my direction. "Really?" She asked. I couldn't help but smile at the childlike excitement. How long had it been since I felt that?

I tossed my hands up in defeat. "I guess we all have death wishes."

She crawled off the bed and crossed the room within seconds, throwing her arms around my neck. "Thank you thank you thank you!" she squeaked. "I'll be very good, I'll listen to everything you say I promise!"

I lightly wrapped my arms around her, trying not to notice how perfectly her body fit against mine. "You might want to change out of this dress. I'll run it by Serefin. We have a long journey ahead of us tonight if we want to pull this off."

She pulled away too soon. "It'll be worth it," she said as she walked to the bathroom.

I really hoped she was right.

CHAPTER 20
Jade

My dark hair blended in with my all black clothing.

Good. The more we blended into the dark night around us, the better.

My clothes were casual and clung tight to my body. I strapped my dagger on the outside of my thigh, a perfect position in case I would need it.

I didn't think about Malachi. I didn't think about the power that rumbled from him in that room. I didn't think about how afraid everyone was as they stared at him.

Okay, maybe my mind had wandered in that direction a little bit.

And maybe I was confused because I wasn't afraid of him. Malachi, the Prince of Shadows and the killer of hundreds, did not scare me.

Malachi and Serefin were whispering to each other

when I emerged from the bathroom, but both eyes landed on me as soon as I stepped into sight.

"What?" I asked.

They both responded in unison, "Nothing," before turning back to their hushed conversation.

"You sure you want to do this?" Serefin asked me. Even in the darkness of the room, I could see the genuine concern in his eyes.

Or perhaps he was concerned for himself. Because we were about to directly disobey the King.

"I have to see Tessa," I explained. "I'll be the princess, I'll move to Fearford, I'll do anything you want. I just have to tell Tessa I'm okay."

He gritted his teeth and passed a look of understanding to Malachi, who just shrugged.

"Don't look at me," he said. "It was her idea."

I knew Malachi was sticking his neck out for me, but it couldn't be that hard to sneak into the human lands.

He had done it before, after all.

I shook the memory of seeing him in the forest before our wedding and I walked toward them. "Okay, so what's the plan? You have to drug me again so I don't expose all of the mysterious fae secrets?"

Serefin laughed. "Unfortunately for you, we need you conscious this time. We don't have a carriage and we won't be traveling on main roads. The passageways through the wall can be dangerous. We need you on high alert."

A chill ran down my spine. "What kind of dangers?"

Malachi looked at me and said, "The kind we really hope you never have to see for yourself."

Enough said.

After a few minutes of Mal and Serefin debating which routes to take, we were out of the castle and on the road.

Nobody saw us leaving the castle. That was the easy part.

I stared into the dark abyss that surrounded us. The fae had no problem seeing in the dark. To them, this was probably just like looking into the jungle during the day.

But to me?

I hated the dark. I had my fair share of lessons learned after the sun had set back home.

But here I was, willingly stepping into it for the sake of my sister.

"You coming?" Malachi whispered. I could barely make out the hand that he held backward, likely after he realized how visually impaired I would be out here.

I accepted it. "Thanks," I mumbled.

"No thanks necessary. The faster we get this over with, the better," he said.

"You really hate humans that much?" I asked.

Malachi huffed. "I don't hate humans, Jade."

I stopped in my tracks. "You're kidding, right?"

Malachi also stopped and turned to face me.

"What? You think that because I'm fae I automatically hate all humans?"

"Actually, yes."

Malachi turned around and tugged me forward with him, nearly causing me to stumble in the darkness.

"I thought you were smarter than that. Not all fae hate humans. Just because you grew up in a place that whispered all the evil doings of fae doesn't mean they're true."

"So, the fae haven't massacred entire towns of people? They haven't used their power to manipulate humans before? I've heard you were involved in quite a few of those doings, dark fae."

Malachi stiffened.

"What's the matter?" I pushed. I knew I should have stopped, but I couldn't help it. He was trying to tell me that all the poverty, pain and suffering the humans have gone through wasn't because of the fae? "Tell me I'm wrong and I'll shut up. But you can't, because I'm not."

"Do you ever stop talking?" he spat. "Or do you just like the sound of your own voice?"

I was about to demand that he answer my question when Serefin stopped dead in his tracks a few paces ahead.

We had only been walking for an hour at the most.

"You hear that?" Serefin whispered.

Malachi's wings tucked even tighter behind his shoulder blades. It was still so dark, but my eyes were

175

beginning to adjust enough so that I could see the figures of both of them standing in front of me.

I tightened my grip on Malachi's hand. He didn't seem to notice.

"Don't say a word," Malachi whispered, barely audible. "And don't let go of me."

I nodded. Fear began creeping into my limps, taking over my heartbeat and pumping adrenaline into every inch of my body. I wanted to reach for my knife, but something told me to stand as still as possible beside Malachi.

So, I did.

Not even two seconds later, trees began rustling to our right. Serefin and Malachi both crouched down in the brush, Malachi pulling me along with him.

I swallowed the urge to ask Malachi what it was. I was too afraid to speak. But the way every muscle in Malachi's arm tightened told me he was ready for it. He was prepared for a fight.

Two figures stepped into the brush just a few feet away from Serefin. He motioned silently to Malachi, who nodded.

The figures were moving slow. Abnormally slow. Eerily slow.

Malachi turned to face me, almost as if he wanted to say something, but he couldn't. Whatever they were, they were too close to us. They would hear anything he said.

But he didn't turn his head. For the few seconds we were crouched in the in the brush, Malachi's breath blended with mine. He was close enough that I could see the shadows of his eyelashes. He didn't look away. Neither did I.

Malachi slowly removed his hand from mine, sliding it up my back. We were close enough, even crouched to the ground, that he could wrap his entire arm around me.

Whatever he was doing, I was sure he had a plan. I stayed as still as humanly possible, but my heart was going to pound out of my chest.

And then one of the creatures screamed, lunging at Serefin.

Malachi jumped and threw me to the side. I landed hard on the ground a few feet away.

The sound of metal in flesh was the only thing I heard after that.

The entire fight may have lasted ten seconds.

"You okay?" Malachi asked Serefin.

"Yeah, I'm good. But we need to get out of here. Where there's two deadlings, there are more."

"Agreed," Malachi said. He walked back over to me and knelt next to where I was still lying on the forest floor. "Sorry, but I didn't want you caught in the crossfire," he said.

I pushed myself to my feet and brushed the twigs off my pants. "That might be the first time you've ever apologized to me," I said.

I couldn't see Malachi's smile, but I knew it was there. "Then maybe we should run into more deadlings. It brings out my chivalrous side."

My breath caught in my throat. Was he flirting with me?

Serefin coughed behind us, and we both began walking.

It wasn't the first time I had been nearly attacked by creatures in the darkness, but as I stepped over the mangled bodies, I had to remind myself to stay calm.

"Saints," I mumbled. "What are those things?"

Dark, skinny figures that almost resembled human children were lying on the forest floor. In the darkness I even thought I saw fangs.

"Deadlings," Malachi answered. "They're savage creatures that want nothing more than to dig their dirty little teeth into flesh. They've been in these parts for centuries, but they're almost impossible to eradicate."

He said it so casually, like seeing these things was a daily occurrence. It was disturbing, to say the least.

"How many more of these are out there?" I asked.

"Are you referring to the deadlings or to mythical creatures that humans have no clue exist?" Serefin answered.

"Um, both."

Malachi jumped over a massive log, then reached back to help me over it. I nodded my thanks and turned my attention back to Serefin.

He took a deep breath before saying, "There are many creatures in the woods. More than you could likely every fathom."

"Great," I mumbled. "That makes me feel much better."

"It's better if you just don't think about it. The wall isn't just to keep the fae out of the human lands, you know."

"Well, that's probably good considering it doesn't stop you at all."

Serefin laughed.

"Let's keep moving," Malachi interrupted in a voice that made me shiver. "We have a lot of ground to cover before we cross the wall."

CHAPTER 21
Malachi

I had no idea how Serefin and Jade were being so calm.

They were talking and laughing as we walked in the darkness. I couldn't even breathe too loudly. I didn't want to hear the sound of an approaching predator or another creature that lurked in the fae forests.

If we came all this way just for a damned deadling to murder Jade, I was going to be pissed.

"We're approaching the vines," Serefin called back to me.

"The vines?" Jade questioned.

"You'll see," I said to her. Serefin and I now led the way, and I kept my eyes open for the beginning of the massive greenery that would soon make it nearly impossible to walk.

"Are we getting close to the wall?" Jade asked.

"Closer," I replied. "But the wall is covered for its

own protection. The forest blocks almost any creature from even being able to lay eyes on it. We'll get as close as we can before we have to fly."

Jade cursed under her breath.

"What?" I teased. "Afraid of heights?"

"Nope," Jade replied. I heard the attitude in her voice. "Just afraid of falling to my death. There's a difference."

Serefin laughed ahead of us.

"Trust me princess, I didn't come all this way for you to fall to your death. You have nothing to worry about."

She grunted next to me.

It took us no more than ten minutes before we were jumping over giant vines and weaving through the impossibly thick greenery.

"Alright," Serefin announced. "This is where we begin to climb."

"Climb?" Jade asked. Her breathing was heavy, and she propped her hands on her hips while she caught her breath. "You mean we have to climb up these things?"

She looked toward the sky, where the vines crawled and ducked around each other at an incline for as far as we could see.

Although I knew Jade couldn't even see that much in the darkness.

"Yep," I added. "But if you'd like to turn back instead, just let us know."

Jade cocked her head sideways. "I'm ready to climb!" she chirped. Serefin gave me a sideways look as

Jade moved forward and jumped on top of a large vine.

The vines were my favorite place to mess around as a kid. Deep in the forest, this place was a mystical playground. The vines were thick enough to stand on, but one misstep would send you plummeting to the ground below.

I didn't bother telling Jade that part.

"You really think this is a good idea?" Serefin asked me as Jade jumped from one vine to another, slowly beginning the ascension to the massive wall that separated us from the human lands.

"Saints, no," I replied. "But I don't think that's stopping anyone."

"Hey!" she yelled. "Are you boys coming, or are you just planning on sitting back all day while I do this alone?"

Serefin clapped me on the shoulder. "Good luck with that, brother."

I cursed under my breath before following after Jade, easily leaping from vine to vine.

Jade was slower, of course. As fae, Ser and I had an easy advantage. But we slowed our pace down, giving Jade enough space to lead the way.

The vines slowly transformed from large, thick logs to smaller vines. Jade noticed this, too, and began crawling on all fours as she used her hands to swing across.

She didn't look down once.

"You're actually not bad at this, princess," I chirped as she easily leapt from one vine to another.

Jade tossed her hair behind her back and laughed. "Did you expect otherwise, prince?"

"I can't imagine humans have much experience with foliage like this. Certainly not in that forest of yours."

Jade shook her head. "You have no idea what I've had to do to survive. Hunting in that forest was just the beginning."

I shut up as we moved forward. For whatever reason, thinking of Jade struggling in the human lands put a knot in my stomach. I knew the humans were suffering, but there was more that Jade wasn't telling me. There was more that she wasn't comfortable telling me. And I didn't like that one bit.

Yes, she had to hunt so she wouldn't starve to death. It was messed up that a young woman would have to do something as dangerous as that to feed her family. But from what I had heard, her father was the opposite of help.

Jade's foot slipped and she let out a scream as her body slammed against the thick vine beneath us.

I jumped forward, easily grabbing her wrist and securing her to the branch. I waited a few seconds before hauling her up to her feet, keeping a hand on her back until she steadied herself.

"Thanks," she breathed, inches from my face.

I smiled. "I think it's about time for you to face your fear of heights, princess."

"Now?" she asked. "I can't even see the wall yet."

"That's because you're human," Serefin answered from behind me. "You can't see it. It's glamoured."

She lifted her chin. The hands she placed on my shoulders to get her balance remained there. "Fine," she said. "But if you drop me, I'll be pissed."

A small growl escaped me. I couldn't resist. I scooped her in my arms as she secured an arm around my neck. Jade was stiff with nerves, but I couldn't tell if it was from me holding her or from us about to launch into the air.

I hoped it was the latter one.

Serefin jumped first, his wings spreading tightly around him as he navigated his way through the maze of small branches above us.

"Hold on tight, princess," I breathed into her ear. And then I jumped.

Jade squealed as my wings surrounded us, hauling us higher and higher into the night sky. It was a good thing Jade couldn't see in the dark. Because the wall was tall, and we rarely flew this high.

But she didn't say a word, just buried her head into my neck as Ser and I made the silent ascension into the sky.

The wall was difficult for most people to see, even the fae. The humans of course would never be able to find it on their own, and they sure as Saints would never be able to cross it. This wasn't the only way through the wall, but it was the best way to not get caught.

Getting caught wasn't an option. Especially for the Prince of Shadows and his new human wife.

I lost track of how long Serefin and I had been flying. It wasn't long until Ser and I peaked the wall, shimmering in glamour, and began our descent into the human lands.

CHAPTER 22
Malachi

I never understood humans. I didn't hate them, but I didn't understand them. I remembered that as we entered Jade's old residence. The smell alone was enough to keep any fae away.

But I didn't tell her that.

She walked in front of Ser and I, just enough that I could watch the bounce in each step as she trotted up the main path to her house.

It was dark. Everything was dark, but she didn't need our help to see anymore. Something told me she had likely walked this path at night hundreds of times.

My chest tightened thinking about her walking all alone at night, scavenging for something to feed her sister with.

I shook my head. What was I thinking? Jade was perfectly capable of taking care of herself in the human lands.

Saints, she had survived long enough in the fae

lands, I was starting to think she could take care of herself there too.

Jade turned on the path, walking up to the front door of probably the smallest house on the entire path. Not a single light remained on, but I knew it was Jade's house.

One, because her scent still lingered here,

And two, because I hadn't taken my eyes off her that night in the forest until I had watched her get inside.

Something inside me wouldn't let me look away.

"Wait here," she demanded as she grabbed the doorknob and pushed it open.

Serefin glanced at me, as if he was wondering if I would listen to Jade or not.

"I'm staying out here because I want to," I clarified. "Not because she told me to."

"Sure you are," he stifled a laugh, but we both remained at the front door as Jade closed it behind her.

JADE

"Tessa?" I whispered into the darkness. The house was just as I remembered it, only with the chill of winter just around the corner, it was much colder.

And messier. As if that were possible.

"Tessa?" I asked again, a little louder.

A thump from her bedroom, followed by thudding footsteps on the floor answered me.

"Jade, is that you?" she asked.

I could have dropped to my knees in happiness right then and there. Tessa was still here.

I didn't have time to answer her question before she jumped into my arms, almost tackling me backwards. I hadn't been gone for more than a week, but saints. Was she getting taller already?"

"How are you alive?" she whispered in my embrace. "What happened? Did you get married? How are you here?"

Her questions rambled on in a continuous flow, and I couldn't stop myself from laughing.

"It's not funny!" she replied, finally pulling away. Although I could hear the laughter forming in her words, too. "You better start explaining yourself!"

"Okay, okay," I said. "I'll tell you anything you want to know. Where's father?"

Tessa rolled her eyes. "I haven't seen him in a couple of days. He'll be back though. You know how it is."

My heart warmed and tightened at the same time. Tessa was never the one to worry about our father's whereabouts. It was always me. But with me gone, she had to step up.

And I hated that. Even though I was so proud of her.

"Who cares about him, though. What about you?"

Tessa grabbed my hand and tugged me back into our bedroom. She sat on the edge of the bed and motioned for me to join her, exactly how we used to sit and exchange stories almost every night growing up.

I guess some things never changed.

I folded my hands in my lap, unsure of where to rest them. I took a deep breath before I said, "I got married. It was giant and beautiful and there were hundreds of fae."

"Tell me everything!" she pushed. But I knew I couldn't do that. I couldn't tell her how much danger I had been in. I couldn't tell her that I had almost been killed, or that I was risking my life by even being here. She couldn't know.

"It turns out Malachi wasn't the one killing his wives. It was all rumored."

"Malachi," Tessa repeated slowly. I became very aware of how the two fae outside the door were likely listening to every word of this. "Is he nice? Is he handsome? Please tell me he's handsome!"

I laughed, and I was very grateful a wooden door separated Malachi from me. But I wanted Tessa to believe the fairytale. I wanted her to think I was okay. My cheeks heated as I said, "Oh yes, he's very handsome." Tessa clapped her hands in excitement. "He's tall and has long, black hair. And he's strong, one of the strongest fae in the kingdom. He has giant black wings, and he's the only one I've seen with black wings. Everyone else has white or silver. It's amazing."

Tessa was drinking every detail. I didn't care that Malachi was listening to this. All I cared about was making her happy. "And he protects me. He's the reason I'm still alive."

"Are the other fae nice to you?"

I thought about her question. "Some of them, yes. But some are hard to figure out. Just like humans, I guess."

She nodded. "And they just let you come here? How often can you come visit?"

I turned my body to face hers and I grabbed her hands in mind. "Here's the thing, Tessa. I'm not sure when I'll be able to come back. Malachi and I have a lot of work to do now, and we might be moving far away from here."

"What? What do you mean? They can't just keep you prisoner, Jade! I need you!"

"I know," I said as I tried to keep my voice from shaking. "But I'll send you money and I'll try to write you as much as I can."

"No!" she yelled. "No, Jade! You survived. You were supposed to die and you survived! You should be able to at least visit me!"

Tears welled in my eyes. "Trust me, I want that more than anything in this world."

"GET OFF MY DAMNED PROPERTY!" Our father's voice echoed through the entire house, loud enough that Tessa and I both jumped to our feet and ran to the door.

"Stay here," I demanded, knowing she wouldn't listen, as I swung the front door open.

My father, clearly drunk once again, was stumbling

up the pathway to our house. Malachi and Serefin didn't even flinch, but in the dim lantern light, I could see Malachi's face. I had seen that look before. He was pissed off.

"I SAID GET!" he yelled again. "You have no business being here!"

"Father, calm down. They're with me," I interrupted. I walked past Serefin and Malachi to stand in between them and my father. Tessa stood still as night in the doorway.

Did he know they were fae? They were using glamour to hide their wings, at least. There was no way it was that obvious.

"I know who they are," he spat. "And I want you to leave. All of you."

I knew he was drunk. I don't even know why I cared. But I clenched my fists at my side, hard enough that my fingernails could have pierced my skin. "We came to visit Tessa," I said strongly.

Malachi moved behind me, but I didn't take my eyes off my father. My skinny, old, drunken father.

"I don't care why you came back here," he mumbled. "Do you understand me? You aren't one of us any longer. Get back to where you came from."

I couldn't believe he was saying this. Where was the father that nearly begged me to stay not even a week ago?

"Father, I–"

"I DON'T WANT YOU HERE!" He yelled, but he wasn't talking to the fae.

191

His eyes were locked on mine.

I was too stunned to move. How many times had my father said something like that? How many times had he sworn he hated me, or told me to leave this house? His words didn't bother me. They were only a reminder of how much the man could drink.

But now? Every word sliced me like a sword.

"I thought you would be happy to see me," I said. I tried to whisper, but I knew Malachi could hear.

My father laughed. Actually laughed. In fact, he laughed so hard he nearly fell over.

"You're pathetic," he said. "You're pathetic, and you're nothing but useless, used garbage–"

The next few moments played out in slow motion. Malachi moved with a flash, fast enough that I couldn't even react before he had my father on the ground, a foot on his chest and a sword at his throat.

"Say that again," Malachi growled at him. I moved to stop him, but Serefin wrapped his arms around me, holding me back.

"Malachi, don't!" I pleaded.

Malachi didn't flinch. He stared at my father, who now cowered on the ground like a child.

"I said, say that again. Tell me that Jade–my wife–is useless, used garbage."

The ground rumbled under my feet. Any glamour he had been using to hide his wings was long gone. His massive, black feathers towered around him.

My father stammered, but said nothing. There was

no way he would say a word with Malachi's sword touching his throat.

Tessa's cry of terror filled the air. This finally made Malachi back away, leaving my father panting on the ground in front of us.

I turned and ran to Tessa, surprised that Serefin had let me. "Tessa, don't be–"

"Stop!" she yelled, holding her hands up to stop me. "Don't get any closer!"

"What? Tessa, I–"

"I SAID STOP!" Her voice was filled with fear and something else.

Disgust.

I looked over my shoulder at Malachi, who just stood with a blank face.

"I think you should go," Tessa muttered. I had never heard her use a tone like that. "I think you should go and not come back."

My whole body was shaking. Was she serious? Did she think I was going to hurt her? Did she think they were?

But Tessa's eyes were wild as they darted between Malachi and me. I wanted her to believe she was safe. I wanted her to believe Malachi wouldn't hurt her, and that he was just trying to protect me.

How could I explain all of that? Half the things I learned about the fae over the last week would be impossible for her to believe. She was like me. She was stubborn and naive and she had grown up believing all the lies about the evil fae who wanted to kill humans.

Plus, she had just seen firsthand how deadly they could be. How deadly the dark fae prince could be.

"Fine," I said after a few moments. "If you really want me to leave, I'll leave."

A sob wrecked through her, and I wanted to wrap her in my arms and never let go.

But instead, I backed away from the door and nodded. If she wanted me gone, I would give her that. I had come here so that she knew I was alive.

I supposed I had at least accomplished that.

"Jade," Malachi's voice boomed behind me. "Let's go."

This time I listened.

CHAPTER 23
Malachi

Nobody had said a word in hours. Serefin didn't speak, but every few paces he shot me a glare. There was no way I was going to apologize to Jade. Not when she was just letting him talk to her that way. Jade was my wife, and her father was nothing more than human scum.

By the time we walked back to my bedroom, the tension was practically dripping from Jade.

"Good luck with that," Ser nodded before I closed the bedroom door.

I stayed there for a second, resting my head against the solid door, before taking a deep breath and mustering the strength to face Jade.

She slapped me straight across the face.

"You selfish, stupid, big-headed son of a bitch!" She sneered. Her face was flushed, and her heart was racing.

Maybe I deserved that. After watching Tessa, the

only person Jade truly loved in her life, cower away from Jade, I understood why Jade was pissed at me.

But even so...

"Did you just slap me?" I asked. Her eyes widened, like she just realized the extent to what she had done.

"You deserve far worse," she said, but her words didn't match her actions as she took a step backward. "You shouldn't have done that, Malachi! Saints, what were you thinking?"

"I was thinking your father is an asshole."

"Well so is yours!" she yelled, "And you don't see me nearly killing him in front of your sister!"

Her face flushed, and her chest rose and fell with every deep pant of breath.

"It wasn't supposed to happen like that," she said, shaking her head in disbelief. "That wasn't supposed to happen."

I couldn't respond. I was watching her unravel completely but I could do nothing but stand and watch.

Jade's eyes glossed over. "She hates me," she said. "She hates me and she never wants to see me again."

Because of me. Tessa hated her because of me.

"All I wanted to do was let her know that I was okay," she continued. Her voice had dropped to barely a whisper. "And now she never wants to see me again." Jade stood there, just a few feet away from me, staring at her hands.

I wished I knew what she was thinking. I wished I

could fix everything for it. I really wished I could rip the head off that piece of shit father of hers.

But she was here. I could at least make her think that this place was better than that wretched home of hers.

I don't know what came over me, but the sudden urge to make her smile washed over me.

"Tell me what you want," I whispered, stepping closer to her. "Tell me what you want and I'll make it happen."

She stared at me with those dark, glossy eyes. As if she couldn't believe what I was saying.

"I want none of this to have happened," she breathed. "I want to be back in bed with Tessa and my drunk father yelling nonsense in the kitchen. I want to be hunting for our food in the forest. I want to be free again," she said. Her voice grew stronger with every word.

"Then be free," I pushed.

"You know I can't," she rolled her eyes. "We both know that."

"But why not? We are about to be the rulers of our own kingdom."

"A kingdom your father—the king—still oversees."

I took a deep breath. "My father has been in charge of me for far too long. I'm not really in the mood to keep answering to him."

"Do you have a choice?" She challenged.

"Don't we all?" I replied.

I wasn't sure when we had gotten so close to each other, but I was standing no more than a few inches away from her. Close enough to smell the cinnamon on her hair. Close enough to see the golden flecks in her eyes.

"This is a chance to get away, Jade. This is our chance at freedom."

She huffed in frustration. "You mean it's your chance? They're never going to stop wanting to kill me, Malachi. They want me dead. Everyone does. And now that I'm the human who married the fae prince, even more people are going to want me dead. Are people even going to accept us as their prince and princess?" She stared at me for a beat longer before looking down and saying, "Saints, I don't even know how to be a princess."

"I guess we haven't really talked about that," I admitted. "I'm sure ruling your own kingdom wasn't in your plans of things to do this week."

She giggled for the first time all day. "No, fighting for my life was pretty much planned to take up all my time."

I smiled then, and I wasn't sure if it was because of her words or the familiar spark that had returned to her eyes.

"I know you think I'm a monster," I said, "but I don't want us to be enemies."

I fought the urge to step closer to her, to comfort her.

She looked me in the eye and said, "I don't think you're a monster, Malachi."

"I could have ripped his head off," I mumbled. I didn't have to explain who I was talking about.

"I know," she breathed. Had she stepped closer to me?

"Good," I breathed back. Or was that me that stepped closer to her? "I would kill anyone who touches you, Jade. I would end anyone who mistreats you."

My words were harsh, but they were true.

A faint smile spread across her lips. "I know that, too."

"Good," I repeated.

My hand wandered to her bare arm, tracing the skin from her wrist up to her shoulder, then pausing there.

"Do you want to kiss me?" she asked me. Her eyes were wide but she did not look away. I leaned forward, our lips nearly touching in the dim light of the bedroom. "I can smell lies, prince," she teased, repeating my words from earlier. "So be careful about what you say next."

A low growl escaped my throat. Jade was testing me, challenging me. And she knew it.

"If I wanted to kiss you, Jade Farrow, I would do it."

"Is that so?" She pushed. "Then why haven't you?"

"You're the one that thinks I'm handsome, protective, kind—" I began repeating from her conversation with her sister.

She punched me in the arm, but I caught her wrist

and pulled her body into mine until our chests were touching.

We stayed there for a few moments, our breath blending, our hearts pounding.

Until I quit resisting, and I gave in to Jade Farrow.

CHAPTER 24
Jade

Malachi kissed me like I was the only thing that had ever mattered.

His mouth crashed into mine in a deep, unbreakable hunger.

My body pressed against his but I still needed more, I needed to feel more of him. He was holding back. I knew him well enough to know that.

I traced my hands up his back, avoiding the large feathered wings that shadowed around us.

Malachi's arms wrapped around my waist, around my entire body, and pulled me closer to him. Our mouths moved together like they belonged there, like they were destined to be together.

He picked me up in a swift motion and carried me to the bed, leaning over me as he laid me down.

My heart pounded in my chest as he pulled away, just enough to look at me. "I knew you would cave," he said before kissing me again.

I pulled away this time and said, "Me?" I asked. "Weren't you the one who swore you didn't care about me."

Our mouths crashed together once more as a laugh rumbled in his chest.

I never wanted that moment to end.

The sound of knocking on Malachi's bedroom door made me freeze.

Although Malachi didn't seem too distracted.

"Go away," he mumbled without taking his mouth on mine. I laughed as I felt the vibrations through my mouth.

The knocking just repeated. "Malachi, I need to talk to you," Adeline said from the door.

Shit.

Malachi's disappointment echoed in his exhale. "Don't think I'll forget about this, princess," he purred before pulling away, leaving me paralyzed on Malachi's bed.

MALACHI

I cracked the door open just enough to see Adeline's face in the hallway.

And enough to see her eyes darting between me and Jade, who was still lying on the bed.

"What?" I asked. It came out harsher than I meant it to, and it showed on her face.

"Father wants to see you," she said, her eyes darting to Jade and back one more time. "Alone."

I ignored the dread that immediately flooded my stomach.

"Did he say why?" I asked. There was no way he knew we had left. I was careful. Serefin was careful. He had no idea.

"No," she responded. "But he didn't look happy. I would hurry if I were you."

I glanced down the hallway, to where Serefin was usually on guard. "Where's Ser?" I asked.

"He asked to see Serefin, too. He's already there."

Adeline was terrible at hiding her expressions. She always was. I could see the subtle fear all over her face.

"I'll stay with Jade," she added, as if she knew exactly what I was thinking. "We'll be right here the entire time, I swear it."

I took one deep breath, letting go of all the fear that was threatening to take over.

"Fine," I said, stepping back to allow her into the room. "But I don't like this. Not at all."

She shot me a glare that said she didn't, either.

"Adeline?" Jade asked from across the room. "What are you doing here?"

"Don't let her leave your sight," I whispered in my sister's ear before slipping out the door and storming off to find my father.

JADE

"What was that?" I asked, sitting up in the bed. Malachi had left the room as fast as he could, leaving Adeline and I alone.

She waved her hand toward the door and said, "Just politics, I'm sure. He'll be back in just a few minutes."

I shook my head, not entirely convinced.

"Don't think I can't tell what you two were just up to," she said, mischief filling every word. She pranced over and jumped on the bed, lying on her side next to me.

"What are you talking about?" I asked.

But I knew what she was talking about. I was certain she could hear my heart racing, even now. I was also sure she could see my ruffled hair, my swollen lips.

Traces of Malachi were all over me.

Adeline just laughed, throwing her head back.

"You humans aren't very good liars," she said. "Did you know that?"

"Oh, shut up!" I joked. "He's my husband, after all. I could think of worse things."

"So I guess you've changed your mind about him then?"

"Not entirely."

"Mmmmhm," she said. "I can see that. Why don't

you just go ahead and admit that he wasn't as terrible as you had expected?"

"Adeline, he—" I stopped myself before I told her that he had nearly killed my father, and he had certainly terrified my sister enough to never talk to me again. "He still has a temper," I said finally. "And a past. And motives I don't understand."

"We all have ugly pasts, Jade. We've all done ugly things to survive. Even the humans."

Her crystal blue eyes blared into mine like she knew something more than she was saying.

"That doesn't mean your brother can't be a complete asshole," I added.

"Please," she said. "I would be a complete idiot if I tried to argue that he wasn't an asshole."

I smiled. "Good, because I really wouldn't believe you if you did."

She moved her body closer to mine and lowered her voice to a whisper, "This might be a bad idea, but do you want to go eavesdrop?" She asked.

"On Malachi?"

Adeline nodded in excitement. "Growing up, there was never too much entertainment here in the castle. But Malachi getting his ass handed to him by our father was one of the more common forms of it."

"You can't be serious," I said, but my smile just grew.

"Come on!" She said, jumping to her feet. "We have to have at least some fun here, right? And from the look on my father's face, he's really pissed about something."

I had to admit, I was curious as to what had Malachi running out of here so quickly.

"Fine," I said, "but if we get in trouble, I'm blaming you."

"Totally understood," she said with a wink. "I'm used to it, anyway."

Adeline led us out the bedroom door, where two new guards had apparently been waiting.

"Where are you heading?" They asked Adeline without even glancing at me. Classic.

"Official court business," she answered. She flicked her long, blonde hair over her shoulder and batted her dark eyelashes.

Damn, I thought. Even I would have fallen for that.

The two guards looked at each other and exchanged a knowing glance before looking back at us.

"Fine," they said. "But make it quick."

Adeline strung her fingers through mine and blew a kiss to the guards. "Thank you, gentlemen," she chirped.

And continued to prance down the hallway.

"Won't Malachi be mad if he knows we left the room?" I asked. He certainly wasn't happy about us swimming in the lagoon.

"My brother gets mad about everything," she said. "I try not to take any of it personally. Like you said, he's an asshole."

I nodded my agreement as she pulled me around the corner and up a grand, spiral staircase. Just like everything else in the castle, it was covered in vines and greenery.

And like every other time we had walked the halls of the castle, the other fae completely averted eye contact.

"Why don't they look at us?" I whispered. "Nobody ever looks at us when we're walking through this castle."

Adeline gave me a knowing smile. "It's because they know who they'll answer to if we ever find a problem with them."

That made sense. "The king?"

She laughed quietly. "Your husband, princess."

I let her words sink in. Nobody ever looked at us because they were afraid of what Malachi might do?

"If Malachi is so big and tough, why does he let your father boss him around like that?"

Adeline rolled her eyes. "See for yourself."

We turned the corner and I nearly dropped to my stomach.

Because we were literally on a balcony, overseeing the same meeting room we had all been in yesterday.

Malachi was standing in the middle of the room, with the King sitting in his throne like the leader he was.

"Don't worry, they can't see us," she whispered.

"But can't they hear us?"

"Not unless they're trying to. And since they don't know we're here..."

"Fine, fine, fine," I said. "Let's just be quiet."

Adeline nodded and we inched closer to the balcony ledge, hiding ourselves from sight as the King's voice echoed off the walls.

"You didn't seem too pleased about my announcement yesterday," he said.

I couldn't see Malachi, but I could almost picture him rolling his shoulders back and lifting his chin before he responded, "What makes you say that?"

The King laughed. It was low and ugly. The type of laugh that made you want to bite your own tongue.

"I know my own son, and I know when he's not pleased with me."

"Is that not what you want?" Malachi challenged. "Does it not please you to have your own son unhappy?"

"I've done plenty to make you happy, boy. I would remember that before you go mouthing off if I were you."

"Mouthing off?" Malachi laughed. "Is that what this is to you? If I remember correctly, it was you who called me here, father. If you would like me to leave then please just say so."

The amount of silence that followed was enough to send chills down my arms. Adeline and I both froze.

"I want to know what was so important that you and your new wife had to leave Rewyth last night," the king finally said.

Shit.

Adeline snapped her eyes to me, but I just shook my head.

Not now.

"It was personal business for Jade," Malachi replied with a bored tone.

"And what makes you so interested in your wife's personal business?" He asked.

"Probably the fact that she is my *wife*, father. I made vows to her. And she to I."

"And those vows somehow make you break the treaty we have with the humans?"

Malachi released a long breath. "We did not interfere with the treaty in any—"

"But you did!" He yelled. Adeline flinched next to me at the sharpness of his voice. "You knew I would not allow you to cross the wall so you did so without my permission. Is this correct?"

The ground rumbled, or maybe I had imagined it.

"That's correct," he answered after a few painful moments.

Adeline's eyes were wild as they stared into mine. Was this normal for them to be fighting like this? Was the king usually this mad at Malachi?

I wondered how many other times Malachi had snuck into the human lands. And how many times he had gotten caught.

Something told me this wasn't the first time.

"You continue to disobey me after I give you everything. I've given you a life. I've given you a wife. And now I've given you a kingdom. When does it end? When does the disrespect end?"

Malachi took a breath. "I respect you, father. This has nothing to do with that."

"Doesn't it?" he asked. "I think this has everything to do with respect, son. Your brothers have no problem obeying me. They never have. Perhaps one of them should inherit the kingdom, no?"

"We both know I'm the best one to rule the kingdom," Malachi responded, his temper began to unravel. "I've done everything you've asked of me, father! You asked me to get married not once but four times, and I obliged happily every time. You ask me to do your dirty work, and again, I oblige. Every. Time. No questions asked. You sit around and use me as your weapon, and I let it happen. Happily. Because you are my father and you are the king. My wife asked me to go to the human lands, and I obliged, because she is my wife and she has given up everything to be here with me!"

"Given up? You really think that human scum had a better life in her human lands? This is an honor for her, Malachi. This was an honor for each of them, even if the first three weren't strong enough to survive here!"

"How dare you talk about them that way."

"They are weak! Humans are weak! Has your past not proved that to you enough?"

"You know who killed them," Malachi demanded. "I know you do. You have spies everywhere in this castle. Certainly you know who is to blame for their deaths."

I froze. Even if we had suspected that the King

knew something, it was bold to accuse him this way. Especially when he was already pissed off.

Adeline must have known this too. She reached her hand across to mine and gave me a 'let's go' type of look, but I couldn't move. I couldn't leave without knowing how this conversation ended.

I shook my head at Adeline.

"You accuse me of murder in my own kingdom?" the King asked.

Malachi paused, as if he actually wasn't' sure how to answer for once. "I just want to ensure the safety of my wife. That's all."

"You're willing to do a lot for this girl, Malachi. I have to say I don't like where this is heading."

My heart was pounding in my chest.

"She has nothing to do with this," he responded. "I simply want to know who I can and cannot trust in my own home."

"You still assume the attacks are coming from within the castle?" The King asked. His voice was cold. The fake ignorance made me want to jump down there and kill him myself.

"I don't assume anything," Malachi answered. "But there has been no evidence of break ins from outside the castle, so the obvious answer is that these murderers are from the inside. And I know plenty of people who may want my wives dead."

"Like who?"

"Like your other sons, for one. I'm sure they don't like seeing me as the heir."

The King laughed again, but it was humorless.

"The rest of my sons have no problem obeying their orders. They know their time is coming. You are supposed to be setting an example, Malachi. Yet for some reason it has been so hard for you to just do as you are told, even with your mother on the line."

This time, Malachi did not respond.

"My punishments for you do not seem to be taking effect. Perhaps we should adjust so you'll learn this time?" the King asked.

Again, Malachi did not respond. Adeline's hand found mine and squeezed. Because we both knew where this was going.

The King turned his attention to the guards. "Go find Malachi's *precious* wife."

CHAPTER 25
Malachi

Uncontrollable rage pulsed through my body in one second.

Nobody was going to touch Jade.

Nobody.

My father sent the guards away, leaving him and I alone in the room.

Except we weren't really alone. The sweet cinnamon scent of Jade's hair hit me as soon as her and Adeline crawled in here.

Not to mention the sound of her heart racing.

I knew she was still on the balcony, listening to every word. But my father didn't know that. For all he knew, Jade was still locked away in my bedroom.

"You really think harming my wife is going to make me obey you?" I asked. My wings inched wider with every second. A predator's defense.

"I think she is your weakness, Malachi. As every

wife of yours has been before this one. When are you going to learn? I've tried to make you learn, I really have. You weren't meant to be like the others. You were meant for power. Can't you see it?"

"Jade is not a weakness." I kept my voice as flat as possible.

My father smirked. "I saw the way you defended her yesterday in the court meeting. Against your own brother, too."

"I was defending myself."

"You lie!" he yelled. "You have grown *soft!* You are not the boy I raised, Malachi. I raised you to be a weapon. A killer!"

I couldn't take any more. I had spent *decades* obeying my father in hopes that he would eventually tell me where my mother was. I had waited and waited like an idiot. But now he was using Jade was leverage, too?

My blood boiled in my veins.

"You want me to be a killer, father?" I asked through gritted teeth. My heart pounding was the only thing I could hear. "Then you should have just said so."

One of the guards entered the room, and I didn't hesitate. I flashed across the room, unsheathing my sword, and sliced the back of his legs. He dropped to his knees in an instance, and I grabbed him by the hair, exposing his neck.

"Is this what you wanted?" I yelled at my father. "You want me to be tough?"

My father's eyes widened, just slightly. Enough to let me know that he hadn't expected that.

Good.

Because he underestimated me. He *always* underestimated me.

"Malachi, I–"

I sliced the guard's throat before he could finish objecting.

"Is that enough for you, father? Is this the man you always hoped I would be?"

"Control yourself," he boomed. "Or there will be consequences."

"I'm tired of controlling myself, father. I'm tired of being told what to do. You want me to be powerful? You want me to be the Prince of Shadows that everyone has hoped for? Then fine."

I stepped over the body in front of me, heading toward my father. Ready to fight him if I needed to. Ready to defend myself and my wife from this monster.

I *was* tired of controlling myself. I was sick of it all. My power rumbled through my body. My wings shadows across the floor, a reminder of how strong I really was.

How *powerful* I really was.

The Prince of Shadows.

"I wouldn't do that if I were you," My father said in a rushed voice. He held his hands out in front of him, as if that would stop me.

As if *anything* could stop me.

"And why is that?"

His eyes moved from me to something behind me.

I turned to see what he was looking at and my stomach dropped.

Two guards dragged Jade into the room and threw her to her knees in front of me.

CHAPTER 26
Jade

"Don't hurt her," Malachi said instantly. "If you even think about touching her, I'll kill all of you," he said.

The power in his voice boomed across the room, but the guards didn't budge.

I should have been ready. How stupid was I to think sneaking around the castle was safe for me?

Adeline had tried to fight them, but it was no use. The guards had trained every single day for combat.

A female fae was no match.

She could do nothing but watch as they dragged me away.

"Malachi, I'm okay," I said to him. But I knew he would do anything to protect me.

I also knew this was a test. The King was testing Malachi to see exactly how far he would go.

All for me.

"You claim she's so important to you, Malachi. If you disobey me, she'll get hurt. And you'll never find your mother. Do you understand?"

Malachi's hands were fists at his side. The fact that his father pushed him this far was astonishing to me. Did he not think Malachi could kill him?

Would Malachi kill him? Was he capable of killing his own father?

My eyes darted to the body on the floor just a few feet away. Fresh blood pooled around it, slowly leaking onto the stone floor.

"I understand," he said through gritted teeth, but the darkness in his eyes said something else. They promised retribution. They promised death.

"Good," his father said. I let out a breath I didn't know I was holding. "But just in case..."

Blinding pain splintered across my back. I gasped for air, but my lungs were frozen. I fell forward, catching myself with my hands before another lash of pain whipped through me.

"Enough!" Malachi yelled. He moved to attack the guards behind me, but his father stepped between them.

Pain was pulsing through me. I could hardly keep my eyes open, but I heard the King say, "Take her and go. I can't even look at you right now."

And then Malachi was next to me, lifting me, darkness swarming all around us. Malachi was whispering something, and then we were moving, but I couldn't stay awake any longer. Pain was splintering through me with every ragged breath that hit my lungs. And I was tired. So, incredibly tired.

Malachi's wings spreading around us was the last thing I saw.

CHAPTER 27

Malachi

The only thing that was stopping me from ripping my own father's head off was Jade.

I had to get her to safety. I had to get her out of here.

And then I would come back and kill every single one of them.

"Stay with me," I repeated. "Don't fall asleep, stay awake Jade. Come on," I said as I ran down the hallway.

Serefin was waiting outside my room, his wings immediately flexed at the sight of Jade in my arms.

"What happened?" he asked. I rushed past him and into my bedroom. He followed close behind me.

"We're getting out of here," I said, lying Jade down on the bed. Her eyes flickered open, but they shut again without coming into focus.

She didn't resist as I rolled her to her stomach and ripped the torn shirt away from her sliced skin.

"Saints," Serefin mumbled. We both froze, just for a moment, as the reality of what just happened sunk in.

My father's guards had whipped Jade.

And they were still living.

My power flared, and the floor rumbled under my feet.

"Go find Adeline," I demanded to Ser. "Bring her here and tell her it's an emergency. Don't say anything else."

Serefin left without another word.

I surveyed Jade's back. The two lashes were bleeding, but they weren't too deep. It would still take days to begin healing without any help, especially for a human.

I couldn't believe I let this happen. Jade wasn't supposed to get hurt.

She was alive, but at what cost?

Were we supposed to continue living in fear, doing whatever my father commanded?

No. I was done with it. I was done with this life. We were getting out of here.

I picked up Jade's hair and moved it away from her tear-stained face. "Just hang on a little longer," I whispered. "We're getting out of here. Tonight."

Serefin opened the door and Adeline pushed past him, "What in the Saints happened?" she yelled. "Is Jade–"

She froze in her tracks when she saw her on the bed. "Is she...?"

"Still breathing. For now," I responded.

Anger flashed across her face. She moved to my bathroom, grabbing cloth and running the water.

"What do you need?" Serefin asked me. "What can we do?"

"You can start by killing my father."

Serefin paused. It was dangerous to talk this way in the castle. People were sentenced to death for treason for far less.

And my father clearly had it out for me. And my wife.

Adeline returned to the room and began cleaning the blood from Jade's back.

"We're leaving," I whispered to Ser. "Tonight. As soon as Jade can walk, we're out of here. I don't care if I have to carry her the whole way."

"To go where? Fearford?"

I nodded. "I can't think of a better place. At least we'll be away from here. My father's uncontrollable. He wants me to suffer and he'll do whatever it takes to get there."

"You think he'll kill Jade?"

I shook my head. "I don't think there's any limit to what he'll do to punish me. He knows we crossed the wall to the human lands, and he knows he can hold Jade over my head. He probably has spies in this castle tracking our every move."

"But you think you'll be safe traveling to Fearford? You need guards, Malachi. You need food and shelter and a planned route. That's days of travel, maybe more. Jade won't be able to make the trip with an injury on her back like that."

I ran my hands through my hair, pacing the room. I was desperate. I hated that I couldn't control this. Every day that Jade stayed here was another day that we risked her life.

I was no longer willing to put her life at risk.

"Fine," Serefin sighed, like he knew what I was thinking. "But I'm coming with you."

My head snapped in his direction. Serefin was loyal, I knew that much. But this would be considered treason, even if he was simply assisting me in my journey to Fearford.

I nodded. "We leave before the morning. Adeline, get her cleaned up as well as you can. I don't want any infections."

Adeline nodded without looking away from her work. Her eyes welled with tears as she stared down at Jade. Adeline would be able to heal her wound enough for travel. That was at least one small perk of being in fae lands.

I placed a hand on my sister's shoulder. "Thank you," I whispered. "And thank you for being kind to Jade. I know she appreciated it."

Adeline shook her head and tears fell down her face. "I didn't mean for any of this to happen. I just want a normal family, Mal. This is so messed up. Jade was... different. She didn't deserve any of this."

"I know."

Adeline looked at me with pure determination in her eyes. "You better take her far away from here, Mal. And don't let those bastards lay another finger on what's yours."

CHAPTER 28

Jade

"Can you stand up?" Malachi whispered. Everything hurt, but he had an urgency in his voice that told me to push past it.

Adeline sensed it, stating, "Don't push her, Mal. Maybe you should wait until–"

"No," I said. "I'm fine. Really."

I placed my feet on the ground and stood up, feeling the shooting pain of ripped skin on my back.

Adeline had wrapped me in bandages and given me a new shirt. My last one had been torn from my body in shreds.

Malachi's hand was at my waist. "Only if you're ready," he said.

I saw the pain that flickered through his features as he surveyed my body. He was blaming himself for this.

He would have killed them all if it weren't for me. I knew that too.

"I'll make sure the coast is clear," Adeline

announced before taking off with Serefin, leaving Mal and I alone in the room.

"I'm so sorry Jade," he said. "I swore to protect you and I failed. I failed you, and I'm sorry."

"Don't talk like that," I said. I moved my hand to the back of his neck and rested my forehead against his. I didn't care that it was an intimate touch, or that I was nearly on his lap at this point. "We're in this together, Malachi. And I don't blame you for your shit family. You can't control that."

He shook his head, not looking me in the eyes. "You shouldn't have to put up with this, Jade. Any of this."

"Neither should you." I moved my hand to the side of his face and forced him to look at me. "But there's nothing we can do about it now, Malachi. Your father is uncontrollable. Let's get the Saints out of here before he changes his mind about letting us go."

He nodded in understanding and helped me stand up, careful about not touching the bandages on my back.

I hissed in pain and squinted as my vision blurred, but I kept moving. If we stayed, it would be a death sentence. For both of us.

"Serefin and Adeline are coming with us?" I asked.

Malachi smiled. "It would be impossible to keep them away."

"Loyal sons of bitches," I joked. "At least we'll have backup."

A few minutes later, we were outside of the castle near the horse stables.

"Can you ride?" Malachi asked. I nodded, knowing damn well I had never ridden a horse before. But we were desperate. And it couldn't be that hard, right?

Serefin and Adeline were strapping bags of food onto their own horses. "Are you sure about that?" he asked. "Because you look nervous."

"I'm nervous because we're about to go on a multiple day trek to a kingdom we've never stepped foot in. A kingdom that may want us dead. All while running from a king who may or may not want us dead, also."

Malachi scoffed. "That's nothing, princess. Piece of cake."

We walked over to a massive white horse. Easily the biggest horse I had ever seen, but it's not like we had many horses back home. "Alright," Mal started. "Hop on."

It was a test to see if I actually knew how to ride. He stood with his arms crossed, watching me expectantly.

I rolled my eyes and moved to grab the saddle, ignoring the screaming pain that followed every movement. I placed my foot in the stirrup that was nearly as high as my hip.

And I stopped. What the Saints was I thinking? I couldn't ride a horse. I couldn't even get on a horse. Even if I was completely healthy and my back didn't have gaping wounds, this would be a near impossible task.

Plus, I would just slow us down.

"Something wrong, princess?" he asked, raising an eyebrow.

"Oh, shut up," I scoffed, brushing his shoulder with my own as I walked past him to the horse that he had claimed as his own.

Malachi laughed quietly. "It's not a bad thing to admit you need some help," he teased.

"Perhaps you should take your own advice."

Malachi ignored my comment but gripped my waist lightly, helping me onto the saddle. His hands lingered for a moment as I settled in, adjusting the seat, before he hauled himself on the saddle behind me.

"Remind me why we can't just fly there with all of your wings and magic?" I asked.

"It's a three-day trip, and we might need all of our strength when we get to Fearford. We have no idea what's waiting for us there. Plus, Adeline's wings aren't as strong as ours. We'll be faster on horses."

I pretended not to notice the feeling of our bodies pressed together. Malachi was my husband. This shouldn't be weird...right? He had likely done this before with dozens of people. This was nothing.

My body was stiff. I tried to keep as much distance between our bodies as possible, but as soon as the horse started moving toward Serefin and Adeline, my back couldn't take it.

"I don't bite," Malachi whispered in my ear. He was close enough to feel the chill that jolted down my spine, but he didn't acknowledge that.

Normally, I would have fought him. But I was exhausted. And in pain. Plus, Malachi was a warm, safe surface behind me.

So, I let myself relax with every step of the horse.

"We're getting out of here, princess," Malachi whispered after a few minutes. I couldn't tell if he was talking to me or to himself. "And let's pray we don't have to come back."

CHAPTER 29

Malachi

Jade fought to stay awake. She didn't have to say it. I could feel her body needing more and more support as we rode in silence for hours.

"We need a break," I announced to Ser and Adeline. "Jade won't be able to ride much longer."

She attempted to lift her head when she heard her name, but quickly let it fall back on my shoulder.

"This should be a good enough spot for the night," Serefin said. "As long as we stay away from the main path and keep alert."

Adeline agreed, and the three of us steered our horses through a small clearing in the thick forest.

It eased my mind that there were so many dangers out here. It would stop any spies from following us.

The ones that wanted to live, anyway.

"Where are we?" Jade asked as soon as the horse stopped moving.

"We're stopping here for the night. You need rest, and Adeline can check your wounds."

Adeline jumped off her horse and hurried over to us so she could help Jade. She grumbled something of a response, but we ignored her as she slid off the saddle.

"You really think this is a good idea?" Adeline whispered.

I shrugged. "If you have any other ideas, I'm all ears."

My sister stared at me for a second before helping Jade to a small log. Serefin was already busy with a fire. It was risky, and he knew that. But Jade wasn't going to make the journey if she was injured, hungry, and freezing.

JADE

Tessa held my hand as we walked through the field of flowers.

"You're leaving me?" she asked.

I shook my head. "Never, bug. I'll never leave you. You know that."

She smiled and kicked the tall grass ahead of her. "Good. I don't know what I would do without you."

My sister was beautiful. She had always been the better looking of us two. Her long brown hair stopped at her waist, and her tan skin glistened under the sun as she knelt down to pick up a flower.

"You know he's coming for you, right?" she asked.

I eyed my sister carefully. "Who is, Tessa? What do you mean?"

"You don't have much time."

"What are you talking about?"

She stood up to hand me the flower that she had plucked from the ground.

But she wasn't holding a flower.

Her hands were cupped in front of her, and they were covered in blood.

"Tessa!" I yelled. I closed the gap between us as she dropped to her knees. "What's wrong? Are you hurt?"

But Tessa didn't respond. She looked at me with a blank face. Her big, beautiful eyes were empty, gone somewhere I could never follow.

"Tessa!" I yelled, shaking her hands. "Tessa!"

But it was too late. Tears ran down my face as I screamed her name again and again. I had to get her home. If I could just get her home, someone could help us.

I picked her up and began walking, but the field of flowers had been replaced by an endless body of water, growing deeper and deeper with every second.

"No!" I yelled. "NO!" I used all of my energy to keep us above the water, but it was rising too quickly. The ground under my feet disappeared completely, leaving my sister and I in the water.

Leaving us both to die.

My limbs were burning. My lungs were on fire. I held on as long as I could for Tessa's sake.

But it would never be long enough.

"Jade, wake up," Malachi whispered. He shook my shoulders lightly, and I was no longer on a horse. I was lying on a blanket on the forest floor. "Jade," he repeated.

"What's going on?" I asked. "Where are we?"

I sat up and took in as much as I could. I wasn't in water. Tessa wasn't here. All three horses were with us, but Adeline and Serefin were gone. Malachi and I were alone and the sun was rising.

"You've been sleeping for a few hours. We took a break so you could rest."

I nodded, not sure I could trust myself to say anything else. Malachi eyed me carefully. "What were you dreaming about?" he asked.

I squeezed my eyes shut and tried to forget. Tessa was fine. She was home, safe with my father. Nothing was going to happen to her. But when I opened my eyes, Malachi's eyes were still locked into mine.

"Nothing," I answered. "It was nothing."

"It was Tessa, wasn't it?"

I pulled my knees to my chest and ran my hands over my face. I couldn't afford to think about her right now. Not when so much was already at risk.

My lips cracked as I spoke, "Where are the others?"

"They went to scout the path ahead, but they haven't come back yet."

He sounded confident but concern was darkening his features as he glanced between me and the forest path. "I think I'm going to go check it out and make sure everything's okay."

I sat up, ready to stand and follow him.

"No, no, no," he insisted, stopping me with a hand on my shoulder. "You should stay here. You're too weak to move, and it's safer for you here. You have your knife, right?"

I nodded and reached for the knife that was still strapped to my body.

"Good. Use it if you need to. And Saints, Jade," he said in a voice that put a knot in my stomach, "please do not leave."

My voice was breathless as I responded, "I won't. I promise."

Malachi squinted, like he was deciding whether going after the others was going to be worth it.

"Go," I insisted. "I'll be right here when you get back."

Without another word, he stood and stormed off, leaving me alone in the forest.

The brutal stinging sensation in my back had faded to a dull throbbing, but it was a pain that radiated through my entire body.

I sat up and reached for a loaf of bread that had been left out. I ripped off a piece and chewed it slowly, thinking about all the times I had shared a loaf like this with Tessa.

Tessa. My stomach dropped at the memory, and I nearly gagged on my bread.

She would come around. I would see her again. I *had* to see her again. As soon as she figured out that she would always be safe with Malachi, she would understand.

Tears threatened my eyes. I was absolutely exhausted. And now here I was, in the middle of the forest, all alone, heading to rule over human lands with the dark fae prince.

Things were just going to get worse from here. We were nowhere near the finish line.

I couldn't help but smile at the way Malachi had defended me. All this time I had assumed he wanted me alive to prove a point to his father or to use me as a way of drawing out his enemies from the castle, but I was starting to believe it was more than that. Malachi was more than the Prince of Shadows I had been forced to marry. Over the past few weeks, he had turned into something more. Somewhere in the dark nights and the lonely glances, I had seen a version of Malachi I never expected.

And I didn't hate it.

I shook my head. I couldn't think about that stuff right now. I couldn't think about Malachi in any other way than as the Prince of Shadows.

Saints. He was my *husband*. Perhaps it wasn't entirely uncalled for if I thought about him that way.

The morning passed painfully slowly. I tried to catch up on sleep, but my mind raced through every

EMILY BLACKWOOD

detail I could remember from the day before. If Malachi thought we were safest in Fearford, then I had good reason to trust him. But hiding in the place that his father told us to go? It didn't make much sense to me.

What was stopping his father from marching straight there and finishing what he started?

Footsteps in the distance caught my attention. "Malachi?" I asked quietly. "Is that you?"

The footsteps continued approaching, but Malachi never responded.

My instincts kicked in. I reached for the knife at my thigh and crouched behind one of the large trees around us. My heart was racing, fueling my body with adrenaline with every passing second.

Who would be out here? Who would know where to find us? Granted I had been asleep for most of the journey so far, but I was sure the three fae would have noticed if someone was following us.

Perhaps it was just a traveler or someone passing through.

I didn't loosen my grip on my knife. Not when the footsteps were approaching quicker.

And it sounded like more than one person.

I wanted to call out for Malachi, but it would be a dead giveaway of my hiding spot. Although when our visitors found the camp, it wasn't going to take them long to find me, as well.

"Jade," A male voice cooed in the silence of the forest. Not Malachi and not Serefin.

But I had heard that voice before.

It was Lucien.

"Come out, come out, wherever you are," he continued.

Saints. If Malachi's brothers were here for us, for *me*, it wasn't good. Especially after we left so abruptly. Had their father sent them to finally kill me off? Had we finally pushed him over the edge?

"I can hear your heart beating, princess," another male voice added. Adonis. I would recognize that cold voice from anywhere. "Come on, we won't hurt you."

Lies.

I didn't move a muscle. Not like it was going to help, though. Not if they could hear my heart beating. Not if they could smell the blood from my open wounds.

I was about to lunge out from my hiding space and slice my knife towards Lucien's head when a pair of hands grabbed me from behind, shoving me into the ground.

"You really thought you could hide from us?" one of the twins said. Saints. All four brothers had come for me.

And here we were.

I struggled under the cold grasp of the twins, but it was no use. Eli easily twisted the knife from my grasp. Even if I was completely healthy, it wouldn't have been a fight. I was an injured female human up against four strong, healthy fae males.

The fight was already over.

"What do you want?" I asked. The twins picked me up and carried me to the center of our camp, where Adonis and Lucien were waiting expectantly.

If Malachi didn't kill these bastards, I was going to do it myself. If I survived whatever this was, of course.

Adonis walked over and knelt next to me, tucking a piece of my hair behind my ear. I flinched away in disgust, which only made him laugh.

"We hate to break up this fun little trip of yours, princess, but you're going to come with us."

"What's going on?" I asked. "What did you do with Malachi?"

"Your friends are fine for now," Lucien responded. "Although they aren't going to be too happy when they come home and you're gone. Which is kind of the point."

I took a deep breath, trying to weigh my options. My back was now screaming with pain, the wounds ripped open during my struggle.

"He'll kill you," I grunted. "He'll hunt you down and kill you."

"Oh, we know he'll come for you, princess. That's the whole point. Plus, we couldn't turn down some quality time with our dear sister, right guys?" Adonis said. The others muttered agreements.

I couldn't believe I had been so stupid as to believe we would be safe. Of course the King wasn't just going to let us leave. He had no intention of letting us make it all the way to Fearford.

I didn't speak as the brothers tied my hands behind

my body. They didn't have any horses with them, which meant they had either walked all the way here or flown. I was guessing the latter.

The thought alone made my stomach drop.

"Ready to get out of here, dear sister?" Adonis asked, walking toward me. I shook my head and spit in his face, anger flooding my body. He was going to take me out of here. He was going to take me far away from anywhere Malachi could find me.

He would have no idea where I went. He would have no idea what happened.

But I had no choice. I had to stay alive. That was all I had to focus on.

Adonis laughed and wiped his face clean. "You want to play dirty?" he asked. He wrapped his arms around me and jumped into the sky without waiting another second. I sucked in a sharp breath. "What?" he asked. "Afraid I'll drop you?"

Once we were just above the tree line, Adonis did just that. I couldn't stop the scream of terror that escaped me as I left his arms, plummeting to the ground.

Except Lucien caught me before I could hit the ground, flying me back up into the sky with a wicked, satisfied laughter.

Fury, terror, and hatred were swarming my mind. I couldn't think straight. Not when my heart was racing so quickly. Not when I could die at any moment.

These brothers didn't care if I lived or died. All they

cared about was hating Malachi. And I was a perfect accessory.

I didn't cry. I wasn't going to give them that satisfaction. I spent the next few minutes thinking about every single way Malachi was going to torture these idiots as we flew.

And kept flying. And kept flying.

CHAPTER 30
Jade

They didn't take me back to the compound.

After what felt like hours of lying in Lucien's arms, we eventually landed in what appeared to be some sort of ancient ruins. I had no idea how far we were from Malachi, and no idea how he would find me.

But I couldn't think about that right now. I had to focus on surviving. Keep myself alive, and the rest would come later.

If there was a later.

"Here we are, princess," Lucien said as he dropped me onto the concrete ground. The structure wasn't complete, and four partially crumbling walls surrounded us.

I ignored the pain from the wounds on my back and scrambled to my feet. Dread filled my stomach. "Where are we? What are we doing here?"

The twins whispered something to each other

before they turned around and left, leaving Lucien, Adonis and I in the abandoned structure. "So many questions, princess. All you need to do is sit tight and look pretty. We'll handle the rest," Adonis said.

"What does your father want with Malachi?" I asked. My voice shook but I didn't look away.

"He wants what we all want, princess. He wants Malachi to step in line."

I scoffed. "You're all just jealous of him. You'll never be a better leader than Malachi. It's not possible."

"Watch what you say. Wouldn't want you getting hurt before your big bad husband has time to come watch," Lucien snarled.

My stomach dropped. Adonis grabbed my arm and roughly dragged me to the corner of the abandoned building, shoving me onto the ground. "Sit here and don't move a muscle. If you try anything stupid, Lucien here will kill you. And he'll enjoy doing it."

One look at Lucien, who was lounging against the crumbling wall across the structure, told me Adonis was telling the truth.

"You're the ones that tried to kill me the night of the wedding, aren't you?" I asked.

Adonis laughed. "Come on, princess. Who else would want Malachi's wives dead?"

I couldn't say I was surprised. "You would do that to your own brother? Why?"

Lucien and Adonis exchanged a glance. "Malachi is no brother of ours."

"But why? What has he ever done to you?"

Lucien pushed himself off the wall and stalked over to me. I tried not to cower away from his fast approach.

"Malachi has been the golden boy of Rewyth for as long as we can remember. It all started with those damned black wings. He's always thought to be better than us. He was always our father's favorite. Our father sent him on every mission, every political tour. He was feared by everyone. And for good reason."

I straightened, trying not to look surprised. "But what does that have to do with you?"

Adonis huffed. "You really don't get it, do you? You humans are so stupid. It's no wonder you can hardly feed yourselves."

I bit my tongue.

"Malachi has it all," Lucien continued. "Yet he thinks our father is cruel and unfair. What's unfair is how spoiled he's been. He's the oldest. The strongest. His power is so rare, he's known across kingdoms. It isn't fair, Jade. We're done with it."

"And your father just allows this to happen?"

"Our father would never publicly denounce Malachi. He knows Malachi could kill him if he really wanted to. It's a balance of power. Make Malachi strong enough to be useful, but keep him weak enough to stay submissive."

My body was shaking. I couldn't believe they were admitting this to me now after all this time.

But it made sense. Malachi had mentioned doing work for his father a few times. He was obviously powerful enough to kill anyone who threatened him, yet he let his father live.

All because his father kept him weak.

And his brothers had been helping him.

Malachi was right to not trust them. How did I not see this coming? Malachi had practically admitted that his brothers hated him. I should have paid more attention.

"He'll kill you," I spat. "He'll kill every single one of you for this. You know that."

Lucien tossed his head back and laughed. A cold laughter, the kind that sent a chill down my spine. "He can try. He's sure tried before. But at the end of the day, Malachi isn't as tough as he looks. That's his weakness, princess. He cares too much."

"About who? *You?* I seriously doubt that."

Lucien's smile turned to a growl. "You humans all think you're so smart. You know nothing. You've known Malachi for weeks, I've lived with him for decades. I've seen him kill. I've seen him slaughter entire villages. But at the end of the day, we're his family. We're the only ones who have been here when everyone else turns their back on him."

Now it was my turn to laugh. "You really think you have his back? This is your version of family?"

"And what would you know about family?" he retorted.

I tightened my jaw. "I know enough."

He smiled again and said, "Of course you do,

princess. Why don't you do us both a favor and just be quiet for now."

"What are we waiting for?"

He took a second before responding, "We're waiting for somebody important."

CHAPTER 31

Malachi

S omething was wrong.

I tracked Serefin and Adeline for miles until I found them both at what looked like another campsite.

"What's going on?" I asked them. "I thought you both were dead. You were supposed to be back by now."

"Check this out," Adeline said, gesturing to the site. "Somebody's been here. Recently, too."

The hair on my neck stood up. "Who?" I asked.

Serefin sighed and answered, "We can't tell. No markings anywhere, no personal belongings. Just this leftover fire and the blanket."

I surveyed the area around us. We were pretty far from our own campsite. It could have just been a coincidence.

But this far into the forest?

My hand moved to the handle of my sword

strapped to my hip. "Adeline, come with me to get Jade. Serefin, stay here for another hour, and if nobody shows up, come find us. Let's hope these people are smart enough to leave us alone."

"What do you want me to do if they come back?" Serefin asked.

"If they're simple travelers, let them go."

I clenched my jaw and let my mind wander to what could happen if we were found. What if my father had sent people after us? What if there was a bounty on Jade's head?

"And if they're looking for us, kill them all."

I knew Serefin understood. He would do whatever it took to keep us safe.

He nodded and Adeline and I turned to head back to our campsite. She followed behind me without saying a single word.

"You can tell me what you're thinking, you know," I said after a few minutes.

She exhaled a large breath. "I'm just worried. I hope you have a plan for all of this, Mal. The humans won't be welcoming of us."

"They'll be welcoming of Jade. She's one of them."

"Not anymore. She's your wife. She's made an alliance with the enemy. She'll hate them just as much as she hates us."

Adeline had a point, but it wasn't something I had time to worry about. Jade in the human lands was far safer than Jade in the fae lands. Adeline, Serefin, and I could take care of ourselves.

"We'll figure something out," I said.

She went back to silence, step after step, for nearly the entire walk back to our campsite. It would have been quicker to fly, but flying over the trees would draw attention to anyone around us.

We had enough of that already.

"What about your mother?" she asked.

The words rumbled through me. "What are you talking about?" I asked.

"You know damn well what I'm talking about, Mal. Father has been keeping her whereabouts hidden from you. Are you just going to give up? Are you leaving here for good?"

I shook my head and clenched my fists. "I can't keep holding onto something that isn't real, Adeline. I don't even know if she's alive. For all I know, he's been lying to me this whole time."

She nodded in agreement. "As long as you're okay with it."

"I can't keep worrying about everyone else. It has to end at some point."

"You're right."

I crossed the last few steps to our campsite and stopped dead in my tracks.

"What is it?" Adeline asked. "What's wrong?"

"Someone's been here," I said. I could smell the presence of multiple fae.

My brothers.

A growl escaped me, my power rumbled through my body and pulsed at my fingertips.

"They took Jade," I said. "They took her."

Adeline already knew. She was running around the campsite, checking for any signs of her. But I already knew what happened.

Just when we thought we were free, my father sent them to kill her.

"I'll kill them," I told Adeline. I didn't recognize my own voice. I didn't care. "I'll kill every single one of them if I have to. They're not getting away with this again."

Adeline looked at me with a fierceness I had never seen from her before. "We have to find her," she said. "We find them and we get Jade back."

CHAPTER 32
Jade

My consciousness was fading. I had to stay awake. Just a little longer, and they would find me. They had to find me.

I had no choice.

Lucien threw a small rock in my direction, making me snap back to my surroundings.

"Wakey, wakey, princess," he teased. "If you fall asleep you might miss all the fun."

My head rested on the cement wall behind me. "You say that as if spending this time with you isn't the highlight of my night."

Lucien stepped closer. "I've always envied Malachi and his wives, you know."

"Really? You don't quite strike me as the marriage type," I joked. Every word took more energy than I had left.

"You flatter me," he responded, still stepping closer with each tiny, torturous step.

I glanced around. Surely there was some way to escape. Some way to defend myself. But aside from a few rocks, there was nothing.

When I got out of there, I was sure as saints going to learn how to fight.

"Something wrong?" Lucien asked. "I can hear your heart rate increasing."

"Just thinking about all the things Mal will do to you when he finds us. It really gets me excited," I responded. I meant for the words to sound strong and sassy, but they were hardly audible. I was too weak.

Lucien took another step, just an arm's length away from where I sat on the floor, and knelt down. His sharp ears and bright silver wings blocked my vision from anything but him.

"Did you think you would be different?" Lucien asked. "Did you think you would be the one human to survive?"

With Lucien this close to my face, I could have sworn I saw fangs.

"That was the plan," I spat.

Lucien smirked. "You really think you can survive against us? Against me?"

I rolled my eyes. "It would have been a lot easier if you weren't all giant assholes."

Lucien didn't laugh this time. "How about this, princess. I'll untie you and I'll give you a head start. You can run as far as your little human legs can carry you, but I'll still find you. Because you're just a human. You're prey. Do you understand that?"

Now my heart really was racing. But I didn't say a word. I lifted my chin, staring Lucien directly in the eye.

"Killing you will be fun. Hunting you will be even more thrilling," he growled before ripping the ropes off my arms with a single movement. "Better get going, princess. The clock's ticking."

I waited another second, just to make sure this wasn't some sort of sick plot to kill me even sooner. But Lucien just waited for me to move.

So, with all of the energy I had left, I got to my feet and bolted.

CHAPTER 33
Jade

I ran until the bottoms of my feet bled on the forest floor.

Dying hadn't been something I was necessarily afraid of. Even when I left to marry Malachi, I wasn't afraid of dying.

But somehow, this was different. In the weeks I had spent here in Rewyth, something changed. I no longer felt content at the idea of dying.

I had to survive, and it wasn't just for my sister. It was for myself.

I stopped running and dropped to my knees. Who was I kidding? If Lucien wanted to find me, he would. Running like the dumb human I was wasn't going to stop anyone.

Malachi *had* to find me. They *had* to be close. I could feel it.

And that was my only chance at living to see another day.

My breathing was loud and my heart raced in my ears. I hadn't run like that in ages. I hadn't *run away* from something in ages. I had typically been the stand and fight type of girl.

But that was the reckless version of me. That was the version of me who didn't care what happened to her.

Footsteps crunched on the dead leaves to my left.

But I was out of fuel. My feet were numb from the pain. My mouth was cotton dry, and the healing wound on my back had split open.

I rubbed the sweat and tears from my face with my dirty hands. If these bastards were going to kill me, I couldn't do a single damn thing to stop them.

"Come here," a voice said. But it wasn't Lucien. It was a woman.

I snapped my head in her direction, and was surprised to see a middle-aged woman, also barefoot, summoning me.

"What?" I breathed. "Who are you?"

She shook her head. "It doesn't matter. I'll tell you all that later, darling. I know where Malachi is. You have to follow me if you want to live."

She smiled as she spoke, as if she were happy to see me for some reason.

Frankly, I didn't care. I was out of options.

I flinched as I stood, and the woman took my hand in hers. Warmth radiated from her. A long braid fell down the middle of her back.

"Where are we going?" I asked.

"Not much further," she said. She did not sulk or whisper as if she were hiding. She stood tall and she held her chin high.

She didn't look fae. Her ears weren't pointed, and she didn't have wings. Although it could have been the glamour that Serefin and Malachi had been using before.

My thoughts were interrupted when a pair of footsteps approached us.

My heart raced. If this woman had just led me to my death, I was going to be pissed.

"What is this?" I asked her.

She smiled at me and stopped walking.

Right when Malachi stepped into view.

"Saints," I whispered. I moved to step toward him, to throw my arms around him, to let him know I was sorry and I didn't mean to leave.

But Malachi stopped dead in his tracks and drew his sword.

The woman shoved me to my knees and pressed a blade against my throat.

CHAPTER 34
Malachi

"If I so much as smell a *drop* of blood spilt from her skin, you won't have time to take a single breath before your life has ended," I said. "Think wisely."

"If you were going to kill me, I would be dead," the woman responded.

She held herself with confidence I recognized only in myself.

Who in the Saints was she?

Power pulsed through my body. Death *wanted* her.

At a single thought, she could drop to her knees in pain and I could end her life.

But the blade was touching Jade. It was too risky.

Jade was covered in dirt and blood. Saints, she looked awful. Her eyes were wild, and her chest heaved with every breath.

"What do you want with her?" I growled. Serefin and Adeline had their swords drawn behind me, waiting for my command and watching the woman's every move.

At my command, they would kill for me.

But the woman simply smiled. "I want us all to be friends," she said.

Jade's eyes were blaring into me, but I didn't meet them. I couldn't. One look at her and I would burn the entire damned forest to the ground.

"And what makes you think we can be friends after you lay your hands on my wife?"

Without moving the blade, the woman took her free hand and placed it atop Jade's head.

"Because," she said. "She is my daughter now, too."

My head spun. The familiar voice. The familiar smile.

I knew this woman.

"Malachi," she continued. Her features softened as she continued to stare at me. "It's been so long."

Power rippled in the air around us. I reminded myself to take a deep breath before daring to say anything. "My mother has been held captive by the King. There's no way you would be out here. It isn't possible."

She wasn't my mother. She *wasn't*.

The woman rolled her eyes. "Of course he's been telling you that, boy. How else would he control that special power of yours? He used you as a weapon this entire time. He had no idea where I was, Malachi. He only made you believe he did."

Words escaped me.

The woman–my mother–released her grip on Jade. Jade fell to the grounding, catching herself with her hands. Adeline was beside her in a flash, picking her up and returning to stand behind me.

I lowered my sword. "Why are you here? Why do you have Jade?"

"Your brothers," Jade managed to say from behind me. Her voice broke as she continued, "They're looking for me."

As if on cue, Lucien dropped from the sky.

I didn't wait this time. He would pay for what he did to her. I flashed across the forest, teeth baring at my brother's throat.

But he was ready. He gripped my shoulders and flipped me, and the two of us plummeted to the ground.

I let my power release, sending pain through every ounce of Lucien's being.

He shrieked and released his grip on me.

But I didn't stop. I let my power flow into his body, breaking down every single inch of his being from the inside out. And I wasn't going to halt it. I wasn't going to reign in my power. My brothers had done enough. They had disrespected me time and time again, but my wife?

"Enough, Malachi," my mother yelled.

I was on my hands and knees, but Lucien was on the ground in front of me. He had no chance at fighting my power.

Nobody did.

"ENOUGH!" My mother repeated. "It's not what you think! He's been working with me!"

"You better start explaining," I growled, "Or you're both dead."

My mother took a deep breath but didn't move any closer. "Look," she started. "Your father has been killing your wives. We all know that. If you don't know that by now, Malachi, you're blind to his ways. I knew he wouldn't let me contact you. I also knew he had spies all over the castle, dead set on following your every move. I also knew that you would be marrying Jade Farrow."

"What does that have to do with anything?"

"You don't have to believe me, Malachi, but Jade is special. I have very powerful friends who have told me to protect her with my life. I couldn't let your father kill her. Not when so much was at stake."

I glanced at Jade, who looked just as confused as I was. What in the Saints was she talking about?

She continued before I could ask any questions. "Your brothers were the obvious path of information on you. They were allowed close enough to know everything about you and Jade, but your father had no interest in keeping spies on their tail. It's not what you think, Malachi."

Adonis stepped out of the forest. "He's right, brother."

"You are no brothers of mine," I spat. "We were *never* family. You think I believe a word any of you say?

It's been decades. *Decades*. And I'm supposed to believe you actually want to help keep Jade alive?"

"We all have our reasons to distrust father," Lucien said as he finally recouped from the ground.

"You knew my mother was alive and living in Rewyth?" I asked.

Adonis nodded. "We wanted to tell you. Honestly, we did. But it was too risky." He shook his head. "We never had anything to do with your wives, Malachi. After Laura died, I wanted to tell you. But your mother swore us on a blood oath."

A blood oath.

I took a breath and tried to calm the power pulsing through me. A blood oath could never be broken. If they were telling the truth, it would have been impossible for them to tell me.

"You were going to kill me!" Jade yelled from behind, pointing a finger at Lucien.

He just smiled. "I have to protect you, Jade. That doesn't mean I suddenly have a love for humans now. You can't blame a guy for having some fun?"

I released my power again, sending Lucien to his knees in pain once more.

"We can talk about all of this later," My mother interrupted. "But the King will come looking for us soon enough. We have to go."

"Go where, exactly?" Adeline asked.

She looked back and smiled at me. "To your new kingdom, of course. We're heading to Fearford."

Also by Emily Blackwood

The Wicked Flames Saga: A Young Adult Fantasy series

All The Crown's Shadows

All The Crown's Embers

All The Crown's Ashes

Fae of Rewyth: A Romantic Young Adult Fae Fantasy series

House of Lies and Sorrow

(Untitled) Book 2: Coming 2022

About the Author

Emily Blackwood is an emerging author of young adult fantasy. She has written three books in The Wicked Flames Saga, and has one book published in the Fae of Rewyth series. Emily enjoys writing about magical worlds and strong female heroines who overcome the impossible.

Follow Emily on Twitter, TikTok, Instagram, and Facebook.

@authoremilyblackwood

CPSIA information can be obtained
at www.ICGtesting.com
Printed in the USA
LVHW112232021022
729801LV00019B/396